· THE ·
ORPHANAGE

· THE ·
ORPHANAGE

Hubert Fichte

Translated by Martin Chalmers

SERPENT'S
TAIL

BRITISH LIBRARY CATALOGUING IN PUBLICATION DATA

Fichte, Hubert
I. Title   II. Waisenhaus. *English*
833'. 914

ISBN 1-85242-161-4

Originally published 1965 as *Das Waisenhaus*.
Copyright © 1977 by S. Fischer
Verlag GmbH, Frankfurt am Main, for the new German edition

Translation copyright © 1990 by Serpent's Tail

This edition first published 1990 by
Serpent's Tail, 4 Blackstock Mews, London N4

Typeset in 10/13pt Imprint by Selectmove, London

Printed on acid-free paper by
Nørhaven A/S, Viborg, Denmark

· THE ·
ORPHANAGE

DETLEV stands apart from the others on the balcony. The orphanage children are waiting for Sister Silissa and Sister Appia to enter the dining room, look into the two deep soup pots, take two eggs out of the hidden pockets of their black habits, crack the eggs on the edge of the pot, let egg white and yolk drop into the soup, wipe the two halves of each shell with a finger, throw the rustling egg shells into the refuse pail beside the iron stove, and quickly stir in yolk and white with the ladle before they curdle.

The red bow of the Easter lamb still lies on the plot of grass by the apse. Detlev looks over to the church yard. Detlev is already wearing his suit for the journey, the one his mother had made a year ago for his first day at school.

After the meal Detlev's mother will come to fetch him and they will travel together through the night to his grand-parents in Hamburg.

Sister Silissa combed his hair for the journey. She drew the parting with the edge of the comb, pressed a curl into place with two fingers. She put her black clothed arm around his head and pressed her face, framed by white, starched linen, against his hair.

— You're not going to be a priest now, after all.

Frieda has promised Detlev a prayer that will convert him into being a Catholic in Hamburg, even before the war is over.

The girls are skipping. The boys are playing cards. Alfred is on the lookout at the door, for when the nuns grasp the handle on the other side.

Detlev's face is white.

— You're looking very pale again today, said the nuns.

Sister Silissa had said:

— Detlev has beautiful large ears.

when his mother left him at the orphanage.

— Your ears are as big as Jew ears, said the teacher, before she struck him across the fingers with the split cane. The cane came apart and pinched his skin.

When Detlev was alone in the washroom – when his mother left him alone in the room at the veterinary surgeon's or in her attic room, Detlev looked at his ears in the mirror. Sitting on the toilet, he pulled a photo of himself out of the pouch that his mother had hung around his neck after the first air-raid.

— My lips are thick.

— I have a curl in my hair.

— My face is pale.

— My chin doesn't stick out.

— He has a receding chin, said Sister Appia to Sister Silissa.

Detlev pushes himself away from the wall. He runs his fingers along the top of the balcony railing. He stops at the end rail. A small bead is lying on the rail. Grey and white.

— It's a doll's eye.

Detlev reaches out. He wants to pick it up. He squashes it. Green slime sticks to his fingertips.

— Detlev has picked up bird dropping, shouts Alfred.

The girls drop the skipping rope and look over to Detlev. The boys lay their cards face down on the cement floor and stand in front of Detlev.

Sister Silissa and Sister Appia step onto the balcony. Alfred hadn't kept watch. The nuns have come into the dining room unnoticed. They hadn't stayed by the soup pots – they cracked the eggs and stirred them into the soup without a single child hearing.

Sister Silissa discovers the cards on the floor and pinches the ears of Odel and Joachim-Devil. The nuns' veils flutter up. The nuns bear down on Detlev.

— If only it hadn't been there, thinks Detlev.

— And we had already tidied you up for your departure.

— If I hadn't looked along the railing. If I hadn't thought: That's a doll's eye lying there. If the bird shit hadn't been lying there at all.

— Go and wash your hands again.

— Then Sister Silissa wouldn't be looking angrily at me now.

Sister Silissa's eyes are half closed. Detlev recognizes every pore in her face. Her lips are the same pink colour as her eyelids, her chin, her nose. The starched, shining linen that covers her hair, her ears, her throat, her forehead, chafes her cheeks.

— If Sister Silissa didn't exist, then Alfred would disappear. Mummy says, Alfred has a sheep's face.

Detlev squeezes his eyes shut. The children become all mixed up together. Alfred's eyes don't move. His cheeks swell. His nose breaks through in the middle. His ears move towards one another.

— If only it hadn't been there.

Detlev's thoughts chase one another more quickly. Sounds, smells merge with phrases, words, fragments of words, letters. Detlev is turning red.

— Detlev is turning red.

He begins to sweat. He'd like to go to sleep. He shuts his eyes completely. Detlev sees the stalk of a hazel nut.

— Alfred dug up the hazel nut and ate it. Detlev admired his mother when she looked sternly and fearlessly at Alfred. She didn't avoid his eyes. Detlev looks at Alfred. Alfred's eyes slide over one another, like grandmother's fold-up spectacles, which she kept in the middle drawer of the kitchen sideboard and took out if she was baking and wanted to read a recipe.

— Are a sheep's eyes as ugly as Alfred's? I said, I like you Alfred. – I don't like him. When he looks at me for a long time, he's trying to scare me. When he's nice to me he's drawing me out. He tells Odel and Joachim-Devil and Shaky everything. They laugh at me. They help him. He wants to keep all the power for himself. He envies me. Detlev hears the whispering once again. It's completely still on the balcony. The wind drops and the nuns' black veils fall back onto their shoulders.

Alfred's voice. In the morning. In church:

— Don't look. Don't watch for the signal. Be humble. If you look, you're a hypocrite. Hypocrites go to hell.

The smell of urine. Hammer blows. Blows on the washroom door.

— That's the devil. He's hammering your coffin.

Detlev opens his eyes. He shuts his eyes. Alfred in the washroom. Alfred in the dining room. Alfred with bread. Alfred with oatmeal cake.

— Alfred has green eyes. Because he has committed mortal sins. I haven't committed any mortal sins.

Detlev opens his eyes. He looks at Alfred. He wants to look him in the eyes. Today is the last day. Alfred looks at Detlev's finger.

— Now Alfred's thinking: You've made yourself dirty. That's how dirty you are, on the day you leave.

Alfred looks at Detlev. Detlev looks away.

— Anna. Will Anna get convulsions when I go away? Anna will go to hell. She said so herself. Anna's eyes are brown. There's no white around them. I would like to look into Anna's eyes always. Anna's eyes are gentle. Anna will go to hell. Soon Anna's eyes will be gone for ever. I'm going back to Hamburg with mummy.

Anna's pigtails are black strokes on either side of her face.

— Anna's eyes have a squint from falling. Her head is as lopsided and twisted as the head of Peter's doll. Perhaps she lay in the ruins. Anna betrayed me to Alfred, because she was afraid of going to hell. Then she was afraid of going to hell yet again, because she had betrayed me to Alfred; then she betrayed Alfred and Odel and Joachim-Devil to me. If I hadn't looked along the railing, I wouldn't have put my hand on the bird shit, Alfred wouldn't be there, Sister Silissa wouldn't be there, Anna wouldn't have told Alfred anything, the devil wouldn't have come.

Detlev sucks in air. He draws up his shoulders. He stretches his back. He doesn't breathe with a gurgling stomach like Odel. He breathes like Joachim-Devil, like Alfred, Anna, Sister Silissa whose shoulders thrust upwards when they breathe in.

Frieda steps onto the balcony.

— Frieda is a real example. Her blonde pigtails. The colour of her eyes. Her ears are not too large, Sister Appia said.

Detlev breathes more quickly. A vein twitches from side to side under his chin.

Detlev is expecting the prayer of conversion from Frieda. She goes and stands in the last row of children.

— Frieda breathes with her stomach.

Detlev can't push the air back out of his throat. He sucks in more and more air. He can't get rid of the air again. Detlev's tongue beats against his gums.

— Frieda is Alfred's sister. Now Frieda will betray me after all.

She had cut his nails and buttoned his braces back onto his trousers when he had been to the lavatory.

— Frieda is an Aryan type, his mother had said to Sister Appia.

— Frieda knows a prayer the others don't know. Sister Silissa doesn't know it. Neither does Anna, not even her brother, thought Detlev at Alfred's confirmation, when Frieda promised him the prayer that was to change him into a Catholic far away from the orphanage in Scheyern.

— If I hadn't put my hand on the bird shit, if Sister Silissa and Sister Appia weren't there, if Anna wasn't there, there wouldn't be a balcony at all. Detlev imagines the church square and the orphanage without a balcony. The railings grow thicker and turn into a wall. The bars change into black lumps. The children bunch together with the nuns and turn into grandfather's compost heap.

Detlev flies high in the air like the red balloon at the

Hamburg fair before the war. Detlev flies high above like
a bomber.

Detlev looks down on the four columns of the balcony. He
presses the railings down with his finger and the balcony falls
off like a block from his box of building bricks.

— I want to play with my box of building bricks in Hamburg.
The walls fall over. Detlev pulls the blocks out of the ground.

— If there's no balcony, there's no wash house either.

Every Tuesday the nuns float through the clouds of steam.
Detlev hears the sound of soapy cloth on the wash board.

— Don't waste the green soap.

Detlev knocks down the wash house walls from above. He
pushes the dormitory away. He strikes the cellophane panes
with his fist. He tramples on each white beam, lays them
bare. He throws out the beds. Erwin's bed.

Erwin screamed like Herod: Not on me. Joachim-Devil's
bed. Odel's wet bed. He bends Alfred's bed back and forward. He snaps it in half. Detlev breaks off the wash rooms.
In the mornings Joachim-Devil hopped round in a circle
there and farted at every hop.

Detlev knocks down the lavatory. He lifts up the slippery,
cold tiles, knocks down the walls they wiped their fingers on
when they cleaned themselves without paper.

Detlev knocks out the doors, demolishes the entrance hall,
overturns the girls' dormitory, squashes the crockery cupboard in which Peter and his doll – Youking – had been
bombarded in Detlev's place.

Detlev forgets to destroy the dining room. He carefully lifts
the enclosure aside.

No one knows what happens in there.

— When they're dead, they're kept in the enclosure.

— Sometimes angels fly in and out.

— At night the devil climbs in and performs impure acts at
the foot of the beds.

Detlev rolls up the garden. There's a hole in the garden.

Alfred had sneaked after him and watched him planting the hazel nut. Every morning before mass, Detlev ran out to feel if it was beginning to grow. Alfred sneaked after him every time. The nut pushed a red stalk out of the earth. Alfred tore it out, broke off the stalk, threw the shell away, wanted to eat the rest of the nut. He spat it all out again. Detlev found the dead stalk, the dried spittle, the chewed nut.

Detlev wants to pack up the church. He's afraid of the crash when the church tower falls down.

— Then I'll wake up.

High above the spire buzzed a silvery enemy reconnaissance plane.

— If there was no orphanage and no parish church, then the whole of Scheyern wouldn't exist.

Detlev raises his hands. The bird dropping doesn't fall off. Detlev rubs his hands together. Detlev clasps his fingers and rubs.

— He's praying. He can't help doing it. He prays like a Protestant.

— Alfred hasn't seen anything. He doesn't shout anything.

Detlev squashes the dropping between his fingers. Detlev puts his palms together. He wants to rub away the green slime without the orphanage children noticing.

— Detlev is a heretic. He puts his hands together with shit on them.

— No. Alfred doesn't shout anything.

Detlev smears the dropping over his hands. He places his hands against one another with outstretched fingers. He crosses his thumbs.

— Detlev prays like a Catholic. Detlev soils our Holy Catholic Faith.

When Sister Silissa said the Ave and the Paternoster, she tapped her forefingers against one another, then she tapped her middle fingers against one another, then her ring fingers, her middle fingers, her forefingers, forwards, backwards, until the prayer was finished.

— Catholics hold their hands differently from Protestants when they pray. If I hadn't put my hand on the shit, everyone wouldn't be looking at me.

Detlev leans against the railing. He wants to stop thinking about all the things that wouldn't exist, if the very smallest thing didn't exist – the bird dropping. He wants to scratch himself.

— Detlev is scratching himself with the bird shit on his hand.

— Detlev has Saint Vitus's Dance.

— Anna's illness is infectious.

— Detlev has to go to hospital for observation. He'll be locked up. He won't be allowed to travel to Hamburg.

There's an itch between his eyes, behind his ears, on the back of his neck. The objects move up so close to him that their corners jab into his eyes.

Detlev squeezes his eyes together. The orphanage children float past one another like the hooting tugs in the harbour.

Detlev sees black jagged spots,

— like the crumpled carbon paper in the municipal finance office.

— Carbon paper must be destroyed after use in case of espionage,

like the partly decayed leaves Detlev had collected beneath the quince tree in his grandfather's garden. He held them up against the brightest spot in the clouds. The little ribs were left, and a few wet pieces. He had never been able to make out a head or a figure in a leaf.

— If Aichach and Steingriff and Scheyern didn't exist, I would never have come to this orphanage.

Detlev's case had been collected by a nun with the handcart. A man placed his mother's chair, her hat box on a tricycle.

They were to be taken to the new room. The new room was too small to accommodate Detlev together with his mother. Detlev walked dowwn the high street with his mother: The stonemason. The café. The cobbler. The grammar school. The town wall. The war memorial. The bank. The primary school. The gauleiter's office. The market place. The other café. The smithy.

— Here is the municipal finance office. You know it just as well as I do.

— Here is Saint Joseph's Fountain. We walked past it on the first day.

— Do you still remember?

— You said we were especially lucky to be evacuated to Scheyern.

— The evacuation is already over. It doesn't last very long. The air in a small town is healthier, that's why I've started work here. But it's no longer possible to find a room for both of us. We must accept that. We've already moved nine times. Moved nine times, Kriegel keeps on repeating. Moved nine times. Moved nine times. As if he had to pay for the move. Then the finance office found me a room after all. If it had been up to Kriegel, we should have gone back to Hamburg right away. It's a small room. The war is to blame, Detlev. When I saw them marching – even before the war – I had to cry. I couldn't bear to hear boots marching in step or see any flags, without crying – with sadness. Do you still remember Mrs Karl's remarks – when we were sleeping in the room above the fire engine. And how proudly Mrs Weindeln looked at her Sepp. He's going to be a real boy. How pityingly she looked down at you. The cold room in Steingriff. The dark road into town in the morning in the cold winter. The water froze in the wash basin. The lavatory was across the yard. There was no electric light. Mrs Schneider said: the others who were evacuated left long ago. – She also said: I'm in the women's organization. – At the Haas's, they claimed you had eaten the quarter pound of butter. I didn't move with you eight times without cause. In Hamburg it's not just the bombs we have to be afraid of. We should keep quiet here too. See nothing. Say nothing. People don't want a mother with a fatherless boy – or with such a father.

— God the Father in heaven.

Detlev looks away from Frieda to Sister Silissa's habit. He avoids the nuns' eyes. He imagines they are angry and fixed on him because of his dirty hand.

— Sister Silissa knows what our dear Lord in heaven looks like. Frieda knows which prayer turns a Protestant into a Catholic. Her brother pretended to be the devil. Pious Anna will have to go to hell four times. Her gossip brought the devil up out of hell. At their consecration in the enclosure Sister Silissa and Sister Appia had their hair cut off. The archbishop rubbed their shaven heads with holy oil.

— Don't think about it. Your father is dead. Be a good boy. Bow when you say good morning to the nuns, or I don't mind if you say God be with you. Don't forget to say thank you and please. Don't be forward. Hold your tongue. There are people who want to set traps for us. I'm on my guard all day long. If we make a mistake then they'll put us before a court and who knows what terrible things they'll invent. You're safest in the orphanage.

His mother stood still on the cobbled square between the parish church and the orphanage. She took off her glasses. She rubbed a finger along the shiny circles under her eyes made by the pressure of the frames.

— The first time we came this way, you couldn't even read. You asked me what the golden letters meant. I replied Catholic Orphanage. Then I had to explain to you what the word Catholic means.

— Now I can read it myself.

— You're bigger and more grown up now. They'll let you see

the whole orphanage from top to bottom. You'll get to know all the Catholic customs.

— You'll come for me every Sunday. Then we'll go to the café at the market and eat ice cream and cakes. You've promised me, that you'll come every Sunday.

— I'll show you my new room, and you can play me something on the recorder, and I'll read you something from the big book of fairy tales. Or do you always want me to be afraid of being given notice – I mean, constantly having to move? Always going from one room to another?

— No.

— The nuns in the orphanage are good to you. You'll sit right at the front in the parish church. You'll be very close to the priest when he sings and to the altar boys when they swing the censers. The boys in the orphanage will all be your friends.

— Why don't we go to Hamburg?

His mother held her coat together at the collar with one hand. She hadn't put her glasses back on. Her face, without the glasses, seemed fatter to him than her face with the brown tinted pieces of glass in front of her eyes, bent over the account books and the registers in the municipal finance office. The mayor and the head clerk came in and stretched out their right hands with palm upturned. His mother didn't stand up.

— A lady may remain seated when a gentleman greets her.

But she interrupted her work and stretched out her right arm. She returned the greeting so quickly, that she didn't put down her fountain pen. His mother's face – when she looked up over the books – was as white as Detlev's face and thinner. The two celluloid rings held the lenses in place. They held the glass so close to her eyes, that Detlev watched to see if his mother's eyelashes brushed against her glasses.

— It's more dangerous in Hamburg than here. Even in the finance department, Gemsheim said: I don't know if I'm allowed to employ you at all.

— You were in a home once before when you were a very small boy.

Detlev and his mother staying in a house where the woman boiled cockerels' feet. His mother had a small box full of greasy, scented eye pencils. In the morning his mother took him to 'The Crib'. He had almond pudding with raspberry sauce. He couldn't eat any more. The pudding and the sauce were stuffed into his mouth with a chipped zinc spoon. The dessert dribbled over his lips, ran down the corners of his mouth and dripped onto his smock.

— You'll never get almond pudding with raspberry sauce in the orphanage. Sister Appia said: We don't have that kind of thing at all. It's war time. There aren't even any almonds for cakes. People are happy if they've got a roof over their heads and a stomach full of potatoes and smoked meat.

— You needn't be afraid.

— Why is orphanage spelt with a ph?

— An orphanage is spelt with a ph, because it's a house in which really only orphans live. Orphans are children without parents or children who have only a father or only a mother. But that's not why I'm putting you there.

His mother put on her glasses again. She stopped holding the collar of her coat. The coat parted. She took Detlev's hand. She pulled him along. She went up to the orphanage door. A girl opened the door, and ran away.

Detlev no longer knows, who it was, what she looked like.

A nun glided down the stairs, her long habit sweeping behind her.

— I am Sister Silissa.

A golden cross hung over her stomach. She had a round, pink face, with thick, drooping eyelids. Detlev and his mother and Sister Silissa stood in the entrance hall for a long time. In the semi-darkness Detlev discovered doors, floor tiles, a cast-iron flower stand, a thick-leaved plant. Large, framed photographs hung on the walls. Detlev saw nuns on them

and a man in a white smock with a white cap on his head.
Children came down the stairs. They wore grey smocks.
— These are orphans. Are orphans ill? Are orphans bad? Do
they have to be locked up? Is it all right to shake hands with
them? When mummy goes away, I'll be an orphan too. I'm
not an orphan. My mummy will take me away again.
Grandfather had shown him the picture of the farmhouses,
that hung above the stove in the living room.
— Are farmers bad? Is it all right to shake hands with
them?
— Farmers aren't bad. Farmers live in the country. In fact,
you must shake hands with them. My father was a farmer too,
says grandfather.
Detlev noticed Odel. Odel the fattest of them all. He had red
hair. His clothes had grey and white stripes.
— That is Odel. Come here, Odel, shake hands with Detlev.
Odel had a damp, fat, cold hand.
— Do orphans have cold, damp hands because they are
locked up together in an orphanage?
— That is Joachim-Devil. He's bad. You must be on your
guard against him.
Joachim-Devil came without being called and held out his
hand to Detlev. The hand was very thin and felt warmer
than Odel's hand.
— Why does Sister Silissa say that Joachim-Devil is bad?
What kind of name is Joachim-Devil? Is it all right to shake
his hand, although Sister Silissa says he's bad?
— Shaky, Frieda, Alfred. They're brothers and sister.
— Orphans can have brothers and sisters.
Shaky ran away. Frieda curtsied. Alfred with the sheep's face
wanted to shake his mother's hand first, but she didn't hold
out her hand for him. Alfred quickly seized Detlev's hand.
Alfred's hand was cold, not wet.
— This is Erwin, our good boy.
Erwin was wearing a green, white and red Bavarian jacket.

— Off you go, set the tables! As quick as you can.

Sister Silissa crouched down. The folds in her habit swayed back and forward. She slapped her knees to shoo the boys and girls away.

Another nun glided down the stairs. She turned round. Detlev got a fright. Without saying a word, she opened and shut her mouth several times. All her teeth were missing. When she opened her mouth, a large hole appeared. When her mouth was shut, Detlev could no longer see anything of her lips. The nun had squashed them right into her mouth. She sucked her lips. The bells of Our Lady's Church, of the parish church, of San Salvator's Church rang outside. A smell of burnt vegetables and of lavatory.

— This is Mother Superior.

A third nun glided down from above.

— Here comes our brown Sister Appia.

Sister Silissa blinked her heavy eyelids slowly at his mother.

— She is completely brown. She has brown eyelashes, brown eyes, brown skin.

— Such a beautiful young girl to have already taken the veil, said his mother and took Sister Appia by the arm.

— Each serves our people as best they can.

Detlev had never seen three nuns together and so close. They were protected from the smell in the entrance hall of the orphanage, from dust and rain by their gleaming white head bands and robes and by their black veils.

Sister Silissa, Detlev and his mother went up the stairs. The stairs were wide and twisted higher and higher.

In one year they grew, day by day, narrower, darker, lower. Detlev knocks them down with one hand.

The steps and uprights of the stairs match the other wood, with the cellophane in the box for the building blocks.

Uptairs, Detlev saw a passageway, doors, a sign with the word 'Enclosure'.

The dining room:

Two long tables with shiny linoleum tiles. Four narrow benches. Windows on three sides – to Saint Joseph's Fountain, to the parish church, to the balcony.
— On which I'm standing.
Detlev didn't notice the crockery cupboard. The cupboard with Frieda's sewing things stood in the shadows. Detlev saw the bloody Christ with the blue discoloured face. Christ hung on a black cross. He was made of wood. He was as large as a man. His skin was white. The rose stems on his head were like the wild rose twigs by the road in the garden in Hamburg.
In the Protestant Church near the town wall there was a painted Christ. The colours were pale. The paintwork showed up every irregularity of the plaster. The Christ there had no ribs under his skin. His toes weren't spread apart like here. The blood there wasn't black at the edge of the wounds. His mother looked at Christ too. She turned Detlev away from the wooden figure. Sister Silissa drew a sweet out of one of the many folds in her habit, held it in front of Detlev's face by a corner of the red wrapping paper. Detlev looked up at the cross again. He felt a pain across his shoulders. His ribs pressed against his skin. He thought he would have to stretch out his arms, like the white-coated traffic police on Stephan's Square – his grandfather had been a traffic policeman before the First World War.
Detlev shut his eyes tightly. He was afraid that the whole rose hedge would be pressed down on him. Detlev didn't see his mother looking at Sister Silissa, Sister Silissa nodding slowly once, his mother quickly handing the brightly coloured Bavarian jacket to Sister Silissa, Sister Silissa quietly opening the dining room door for his mother.
When Detlev turned away from the green face again, his head came up against the black cloth of Sister Silissa's habit. His mother had disappeared. Sister Silissa smiled at him, squatted down in front of him, clapped her hands.

Detlev ran to the door. Nuns and children came with plates, cutlery, tumblers. Detlev pulled himself up by the handle. Sister Appia pushed the door shut. Detlev hung on to the handle with outstretched arms. The lipless Mother Superior brought him a picture of a saint. She waved the sheet of paper up and down in front of his face. Detlev's tears mingled with snot and saliva. Sister Appia's arm grew tired. She leant her back against the door. When she turned round, Detlev managed to pull the door open. Sister Appia pushed the door shut again. Detlev let himself fall to the ground. He curled up, struck out at the people around him with his feet, struck his head against the wall. Mother Superior and Sister Appia set him on his feet.

Sister Silissa had stepped underneath the wooden Christ. The tables were not covered in plates and cutlery and tumblers. All the orphans stood beside the benches and held their hands tight together. Sister Silissa shut her eyes and spoke in a foreign language. The orphans spoke quietly along with her.

Detlev remembers that the wall behind the green, blue, black-red, white Christ became transparent and he saw his mother down in the square in front of the church. She stumbled over the uneven stones. She was crying. The rims of her eyelids were red, swollen from crying. Her face became wet and shiny. The tears dropped onto her coat. His mother said out loud — Detlev, Detlev.

The nuns crowded towards her and wanted to hold her mouth shut. She was covered by their black habits. She freed herself. She wanted to get through the door. The door was locked. Detlev didn't try to run away a second time.

He knew he wouldn't succeed. They would all stop speaking the ununderstandable language.

— They would stand in front of the door. If I get through the door, Kriegel will catch me. If Kriegel doesn't catch me, the policeman in Hamburg will catch me. If the policeman doesn't find me, the Führer will get me.

— If there was no Kriegel, if there was no policeman, if there was no Führer, then I would have run away.

Behind Sister Silissa, behind the wooden Christ he saw his mother beating against the main door. Behind his mother he saw his grandmother and grandfather, surrounded by burning quinces, gooseberries, redcurrants.

The soup was the colour of rusty water. It tasted of polish and soot. There were small pale green pellets in the bread.

— It's mould. Mould is good for you.

After the meal the nuns laid cellophane pictures on the linoleum table top in front of Detlev, as well as sweets and picture books with brown finger marks on the edges. The boys wanted to play ludo with him.

— Come over here. We're playing 'German regions and provinces'.

He was to play draughts.

— Do you want to play nine men's morris with us?

He sat down beside the big boys who were doing school exercises. In front of him sat a girl with a round wooden frame that had white cloth stretched across it. She pushed the needle through the fabric from above and pulled the violet thread down.

— That will be the magnificent mantle of the Virgin Mary.

The nuns walked through the dining room, tugged at ears, crossed out figures, laughed, undid a knot in the thread.

The nuns shooed the girls and boys out of the dining room. Sister Silissa enveloped Detlev in her black habit, gave him a sweet, went with him to the dormitory, grasped the cold iron posts, said:

— This is your bed.

Detlev folded his jacket and laid it over the bed frame, then his shirt, his undershirt, his vest. He slipped on the nightshirt.

Sister Silissa nodded to him.

— Let nothing impure be seen.

Then he unbuttoned his boots, put them under the strange bed, pulled off his long stockings, the trousers with the straps, his underpants. He lay down on his side. The feather bed squashed him. He pulled his knees up to his chin.

Sister Silissa rattled her rosary. She clasped her hands, raised her right hand, drew the hand down through the air, and from right to left.

Darkness.

Breathing. Detlev's breathing. The breathing of the others. Detlev pushed his shoulders upwards. The others breathed evenly.

Detlev tried to hear whether they were sleeping. His mouth filled with saliva. He had to stop breathing and swallow the saliva.

Detlev's bed was being shaken. Detlev opened his eyes. The dormitory was white. The moonlight picked out the white-washed walls and the feather beds. No one was standing in front of Detlev's bed, no one behind the bed, no one on the right, no one on the left. An arm reached out of the next bed to the metal bars behind Detlev's head and shook them.

— Are you asleep yet?

— Yes.

— Give me the sweet.

— I don't have a sweet.

— Sister Silissa gave you one.

— I don't know where it is.

— Give it to me. I'll protect you too.

— I've lost it.

— Look for it. I'm Alfred.

The blanket on the next bed was thrown aside. There was a smell of feet, of sour milk and of hair. Alfred looked under Detlev's pillow. He put his hand in the pocket of Detlev's night shirt.

— That's where you've got the sweet.

— Let the new boy keep the sweet.

— The new boy is my friend. I'm protecting him.

— How are you going to protect him. You're even afraid of us, Alfred.

— The nuns will beat you black and blue, Alfred.

Alfred covered up his feet again, the smell of sour milk and of hair.

— The new boy is my best friend. He'll see that it's better if I protect him. He gave me the sweet as a present.

— I know a joke. The Reich Field Marshall . . .

— The enemy is listening.

— Detlev isn't an enemy.

— You don't know that.

— The three of them are walking past a farm.

— Which three?

— Let's say Xaver, Franz, Joseph.

— Joseph goes into the farmhouse to get something to eat. And he doesn't come back. Then Franz and Xaver see Joseph being carried out on a stretcher.

Detlev doesn't remember how the joke ended. Detlev remembers that the orphanage boys laughed under their blankets.

Alfred asked:

— What's your name?

— Detlev.

— Nothing else? How old?

— Seven.

— Where are you from?

— Hamburg.

— Do you belong to the Holy Catholic Church?

— I'm sure I would like to.

— Is your mother in the Party?

— Sure.

— Are you a Protestant?

— I don't know.

— Why don't you stay in Hamburg?

— Mummy says, because of the bombs.

— I don't believe that.

— If mummy says so, then it's true.

— Where is your father?

— I don't know that.

— In the war?

— No. Dead.

— In the war? Killed?

— I don't know.

— How do you know that he's dead.

— Mummy said so.

— What if she's lying?

— She doesn't tell lies.

Again Detlev hears only breathing. A black figure with white cloths on its head pattered in.

— Quiet now. Go to sleep, all of you. You go to sleep now too, Detlev.

The white cloths turned away. Sister Silissa didn't shut the dormitory door. The corridor grew as dark as the nun's habit. Whispering again:

— Mrs Weindeln found a half-rotted leaf in Aichach. There were holes in the leaf. All the holes together looked like the face of Lord Jesus and like Lord Jesus's hand raised in blessing. It's a miracle.

Alfred asked:

— Why have you been put in the orphanage?

— My mother can't get a room for both of us.

— Even though she's in the Party?

— Perhaps she isn't in the Party.

— Does your mother work in Scheyern?

— For the town council.

— In the town hall?

— Yes.

— If she does her work properly, she would have found a room for both of you. Perhaps there's something else wrong with her? Why do you have such big ears?

— I don't have big ears. You've got big ears yourself.

Detlev heard the breathing again. Then there was talk about Kriegel, who beat the Poles in the town hall cellar so badly with a whip full of metal stars, that their screams could be heard during Holy Mass.

— The Poles should give Kriegel himself a beating instead.

— They can't do that, because he's a policeman. They're prisoners of war.

— What if they do it anyway?

— We should leave out some coins that have been in a fire: There, Mr Kriegel, we've put some money on the window-sill for you. When he picks them up, he burns his fingers, so that he can't beat any more Poles.

— And after that the nuns would be arrested, because they're responsible for everything we do. The Holy Catholic Church is exposed to great persecution in these years.

— In Poland the Poles cut German prisoners of war in half with band saws.

— We have to choose between final victory or Bolshevik chaos.

The visit to Hamburg. Detlev, his mother arrived in Hamburg before sunrise. The central railway station was painted in camouflage colours. A placard with a picture of a slant-eyed man hung on every lamp post.

— Wheels roll for victory.

— In Lauterbach a farmhand cut the throats of the farmer and his wife and their seven children. They were all asleep.

— If someone from the Party arrests a sister and executes her, he has no more peace by day or by night. By day she would appear to him and sit beside him at table and snatch the vegetables and meat and eggs from his fork and at night she would lie in his bed with a bright glow around her

head; blood would burst from her wounds, and she would
constantly weep when he wants to sleep.

— He won't be put out by a few tears from a dead sister.

— They were going to take away a sister from San Salvator.
She made the sign of the cross and the people from the secret
police ran away, foaming at the mouth.

— Alfred, you go and lay down the money for Kriegel. It was
your idea.

— Then the Holy Catholic Church will suffer new persecu-
tions. Perhaps they'll take away the whole orphanage and
shoot us all.

— But if it's enough to make the sign of the cross in defence.

— Come on, Alfred.

— I want to go to sleep now.

There was a rustling at the door.

A nun came closer. She stood in the moonlight. She didn't
switch on the light. She moved her lips without speaking.
She turned the pages of her prayer book. She stepped back.
She dissolved in the blackness of the corridor.

The breathing around Detlev grew louder and more
regular.

— No one's looking at me in the dark any more.

Detlev saw his mother in front of him in the new room he
didn't know. He saw the Nivea oil bottle and the black box
with the perfumed eye pencils. He saw the spectacles lying
on the night table, beside them the red-bound prayer book.

— They're Protestant prayers.

The book of fairy tales, the comb, the hairpins.

It grew dark above Detlev's bed. He didn't dare move. He
didn't know whether it was the shadow of a dead or a living
nun or the shadow of a telegraph pole in the garden of the
orphanage.

— Now I shall eat only once more in the orphanage.

In the morning after breakfast the orphanage children
walked to early mass in pairs. They walked quickly across

the church square shepherded by the nuns. They entered
the church through the side door, bumping against the door
posts. The pillars were close together. Detlev began to feel
dizzy when he leant his head back and looked up at the
vaulting. Above, the pillars spread out like the rhubarb
stalks on the rhubarb leaves in grandfather's garden, which
Detlev, lying on his back on the cinder path, had looked at
from below before the war began. Detlev knelt down like the
others. Sister Silissa, kneeling in the gallery, nodded down to
him. Above, behind Detlev, the organ shook and rattled like
a watering can being dipped into a barrel. Scales and pebbles
rub against the sides.
Two boys in white shirts which reached down to the ground
swung silver censers. In Hamburg boys swung smoking
containers made of tin cans on stiff wires.
— I'll never be an altar boy.
The parish priest wore a green embroidered chasuble.
— Now you'll never be a priest, Sister Silissa had said.
The altar boys picked up the golden bells from the carpet
on the altar steps and shook them. The parish priest sang
in the foreign language. As he sang Detlev thought of a hen
that had got lost in the raspberry bushes. He thought of the
noise of cars in the night, far away, when his grandfather had
stepped out of the air-raid shelter with Detlev during a pause
in the raid. The people in the church stood up. Detlev stood
up. They knelt down. Detlev knelt down. When they sang,
he tried to guess the notes in advance and to merge with the
voices of the orphanage children. When Alfred made the
sign of the cross beside him, Detlev raised the thumb of his
right hand to his forehead, brought it down to his stomach,
touched his left shoulder, his right shoulder. The smoke
from the silver censers smelt like the bitter almond tasted,
which his grandmother mixed into the semolina cake.
— We need seven eggs.
— Seven eggs.

He had sucked at the little bottles of flavouring, when his grandmother turned her back, before he and his mother had been evacuated to Scheyern. The altar boys carried a heavy book from one side of the altar to the other. The parish priest climbed round a pillar. He stopped in a barrel, which was stuck to the pillar. He spoke in German of Our Saviour and Lord Jesus Christ and of our great Father, the Almighty. The parish priest grew tired while he spoke. His words tapered off, so that Detlev could no longer understand them.

Detlev remembers that he began to fall asleep under the barrel, between the giant, grey rhubarb stalks. The orphanage children's hands fell from their knees. Their chins fell onto their collars. The black folds in the nuns' veils were still, as though they were covering coffins or tailors' dummies or bean stalks.

Detlev discovered a picture in one of the arches behind the altar. A man bent down beside Christ and looked for something on the ground. Detlev thought of the fairy tale with the cook who wants to box the ears of the kitchen boy. Both fall asleep because the princess has pricked herself on the spindle.

The priest began to shout:

— Our Father. . . The kingdom of God and the kingdom. . . the Reich. . .

The boys thrust their noses forward. The nuns smoothed down their veils. The priest climbed down from the barrel. The altar boys opened small doors in one of the pillars. The priest opened a small door in the altar. He pulled out golden objects. The altar boys brought him a silver dish. The parish priest washed his hands. They held out a towel for him, and he dried himself with it. The altar boys shook the golden bells again. The priest knelt before the altar. He raised pointed golden utensils high in the air. People from the nave moved closer to the altar, knelt down on a long, narrow shelf. Detlev watched them from the side. They stretched

out their tongues. The parish priest laid little round leaves
on their tongues. The people closed their eyes. They leant
backwards.

They stood up with their hands pressed together – palm
against palm, outstretched finger against outstretched finger. They pushed back between the benches. The teacher
swayed as she walked. She didn't open her eyes. She smiled.
— She likes the taste of the little leaf on her tongue so
much.

The organ creaked and groaned. Detlev was afraid it would
fall down out of the rhubarb arches. The nuns stood up. The
orphanage children ran to school. Detlev together with Odel.
They went into a classroom.

Detlev is beginning to get the order of the mass muddled.
He mixes up the movements of the altar boys and the parish
priest. He has forgotten when the congregation made the
sign of the cross. He can no longer repeat the syllables of
the foreign words he learned off by heart.

He thinks of the second box of building blocks in Hamburg,
of the blocks without turrets and arches, from which a building like the orphanage can't be constructed.

The box contains sixteen uniform cubes. A sixteenth of a
landscape or a swimming pool or a royal procession is stuck
to each side. Detlev was four years old when he got the box of
square blocks for his birthday. He quickly understood how to
play with it: He only had to put together the landscape or the
swimming pool, then he could make one picture after another
appear, by turning over one row after another four blocks at
a time. Detlev can smell the shiny paper on the blocks, as
he thinks that there would be no picture of a landscape, or
a swimming pool or a royal procession, if he had never come
to the orphanage.

The views of the towns of Scheyern and Aichach and
Steingriff are turned over like the picture sections on the
big blocks.

Detlev in front of the town hall steps.
— I want to see mummy.
Detlev inside the town hall.
— I want to see my mummy.
— Are you Detlev?
— Yes.
Detlev on the first floor.
Two men in uniform, with leather straps, stood motionless in front of the banqueting hall.
Detlev watched to see if they rolled their eyes or their eyelashes blinked or if they swallowed saliva. They both looked at him. A fly settled on the nose of one of the soldiers. He didn't hit out at it with his hand or the rifle or the leather strap. He pushed out his lower lip and blew the fly away.
The hall was decorated with flags and red and brown drapes. A man lay in the middle of the hall. Tubs with azaleas and laurel trees framed the figure. Detlev came closer to the man. He smelt of orphanage bread. The man's face was yellow. His eyes were closed. He wasn't swallowing any saliva. His eyelashes didn't move. Flies settled on his forehead and on his eyelids. They ran across his mouth. Detlev forgot that he wanted to see his mother.
Detlev on the stairs.
Three steps at a time.
Detlev at the bottom.

Sunday afternoon.
Detlev waited for his mother – as he waits for her now. Washed. Combed. He was wearing the Bavarian jacket. It was vespers. The enamel mugs were clattering against one another in the kitchen. Wasps were crawling over the thick slices of bread with their thin coating of jam. The hunger which Detlev usually felt at this time of day was being pushed away by a cushion of air.

He was frightened of not recognizing his mother again. When she came, she was completely his mother. He recognized every hair, every wrinkle, every movement of the throat again.

His mother talked about her new room, which he was going to see right away – as they walked past Saint Joseph's Fountain. There were short flurries of rain. The wind blew the rain against the tree trunks.

— I have a large wardrobe in the hallway. To cover me at night there's a huge feather bed, which half suffocates me. I have to fetch the water downstairs. The people are very pleasant and friendly. They asked about you. I'm sure it'll be all right for quite a long time. The veterinary surgeon lives downstairs. The street in front of the house is often blocked by sheep. The veterinary surgeon has to inspect the flock. From the window I have a view of the meadows by the river.

Detlev's mother told him that his grandmother and grandfather had written to her of heavy air raids on Hamburg.

Detlev and his mother walked across the market place. Lamp posts and platforms had been set up for the gauleiter's funeral ceremony. The wet flags stuck to the poles.

— I know what orphans are now. They all wear grey-striped clothes. And they don't get any sweets. They say sweetie instead of sweet like other people. They are very envious, and most are stronger than I am, and they want to protect me.

— Detlev, that's stupid. You mustn't draw conclusions about everyone from a few exceptions. Because you're in the orphanage in Scheyern now, you mustn't draw conclusions about all orphans from the Scheyern orphanage and its children. That's just as silly as if you said: A mother is someone who lives in a small room and only visits her son once a week. It's only circumstances that force us to be like that.

Detlev and his mother sat down in the café next to the market arcade. They sat opposite one another.

— I didn't mean to say that at all.

— Perhaps what I've been telling you about my new room is a little exaggerated.

They were silent. The silence prevented Detlev from saying what he wanted to tell his mother. She took off her glasses. Without the lenses her eyes looked like brown ashes. Rough, brown, sticky pieces of coke, which his grandfather put down between the larkspur and the peonies, to make the path firmer.

The eyes were different from how he had imagined them for a whole week.

What he had been afraid of, what he had overlooked at first, had happened. His mother had changed. She had become different and he didn't know why.

He looked away from her to the pink ice cream.

— I am with mummy. That's mummy. That's mummy.

— The gauleiter has died.

— The day before yesterday I was in the town hall after school. He was laid out. The two soldiers in front of the body had little swords stuck on the end of their rifles.

Detlev's mother put on her glasses again. Detlev tried to remember what her eyes had looked like just a few seconds before – before they had been covered by the lenses again. He was unable to.

— Alfred said that Kriegel beats the Poles.

— You mustn't say that out loud.

His mother looked over her shoulder. The waitress clicked the ice cream tongs. She wasn't listening. A couple was sitting at the window. They couldn't have heard anything, because Detlev and his mother couldn't understand what they were saying. The puffy cheeked man was talking insistently to the woman.

— The orphans also told a joke.

— I don't want to hear it. You shouldn't pay any attention to such jokes.

— I didn't understand why they laughed.

— Forget it completely. Don't listen. Just don't say anything. If they ask you, say: I didn't see or hear anything. Say: It's the Poles' own fault. Why don't they work? Say: Anyone who wants to work, has enough to eat and isn't beaten with a whip.

— That's true.

— If we behave carelessly, we can even be caught out here too. I was so afraid in Steingriff that day when you turned up with the medals. Where on earth did you get those medals?

— I don't know. Our captain discovered them. Sepp hid them in a little wooden house. Anton handed them out if we had been brave. Later I became a captain too.

— If someone had been watching you! We could still all end up goodness knows where. Where on earth did the medals come from? A whole pile of them! – There were enough to decorate a whole regiment.

— It was nice in Steingriff. We rode in a gig. I got a medal for my bravery.

— Thank God I forced you to throw it away in the wood in time. I should have reported it to the police or the local Party branch. I still don't understand how you could have come upon such a huge pile of medals.

— Perhaps they had already been used?

— Already used! Don't get mixed up in anything. There are some people who only want to draw you out. They'll say any old thing just to hear how you respond. Perhaps the medals were nothing but a trap, and the joke and the story about Kriegel. Don't laugh at any joke. And Kriegel is a friendly man really. He's a little bad-tempered on the surface. He has a wife and children, he's even got grandchildren already. A country policeman doesn't have an easy life. Don't believe anything. Don't let anyone try to draw things out of you.

— Now Alfred won't ask me any more questions ever again. When mummy fetches me this time, she'll never bring me back again.

— They're nice to you in the orphanage, aren't they?

— Sister Silissa gives me a sweet before I go to bed. On Wednesday I had stomach ache, so I was given an egg cup full of red wine. It tasted bitter.

— You're seeing lots of new things and you're together with children of the same age. People get on well in such a community.

— A few are allowed to confess and go to Holy Communion. If I pray a lot and don't sin much, perhaps I'll be allowed to go to Holy Communion later too.

His mother took off her glasses again. Detlev looked carefully at the lines in his mother's face. He wanted to remember everything exactly. He wanted to know what had changed in her face. The following Saturday he wanted to check what new changes there had been.

— Mummy's afraid. She's afraid of the bombs. But then she's afraid of something else. Of what?

— I love you as much as the Virgin Mary in heaven above.

— Detlev, you mustn't make such a comparison. You're a Protestant. You're not a Catholic.

On Monday Alfred said over the mouldy bread:

— She will lead you astray. Don't listen to her. Listen to me, because now you're in the orphanage. You mustn't say: My mother is as beautiful and as good and as gentle as the Virgin Mary. That's heresy. What did you do after you had eaten?

— When the rain stopped we went for a walk by the town wall. Then my mummy showed me her new room. Then we ate goat soup at the veterinary surgeon's. He said to his housekeeper: This goat soup could revive the dead.

— And then. . .

— Then we ate oatmeal cakes upstairs in mummy's room. Then my mummy washed me.

— Washed you again?

— Yes. She cut my nails too. Then I went to bed. It was

only a mattress on the floor. But once a week that's all right, my mummy said. Then she read me a long fairy tale. Then we drank coffee together again and ate oatmeal cakes. On Saturday afternoon I played my recorder. Then I didn't want to go back to the orphanage at all. But my mummy was afraid of bringing me back too late. We both ran because she wanted to be on time.
— Are you frightened of the orphanage?
— No.
— Are you frightened of me? You don't need to be. I'll protect you. What kind of cake is that – oatmeal cake?
— My granny sent it from Hamburg. She put the recipe in with it. Instead of flour you use oatmeal.
— Give me your bread and jam. You had oatmeal cake yesterday.
— There's mould on my bread.
— Mould is good for the digestion. In times like these we mustn't complain about every little thing.
Detlev noticed how Alfred pushed out his lower lip until the lower lip began to hang down. Alfred looked at Detlev. Detlev looked away. Detlev pushed the bread and jam over to Alfred.

Detlev's mother had waited between the parish church and the orphanage, until he had caught up.
— Don't dawdle so.
Then she wrapped her blue coat around Detlev, pressed Detlev against her, and said into the blue coat:
— What with all my fears and worries, I didn't even manage to hug you.

In the parish church, behind the bench where Sister Silissa knelt, hung another oil painting.

When instead of the small, hoarse priest, the tall, pale one said mass, Detlev felt as if sand was trickling down his back. He turned round to look at the oil painting. A dark green meadow was painted inside the black moulding of the frame.

Clouds of incense from the altar blew into the niche where the oil painting hung.

The meadow was crowded with people. On the horizon they were as small as black lice, sticking to field poppies in big clumps, towards the front the people became larger and larger.

— It's called perspective. Leonardo da Vinci invented it. He was Italian, his name is spelt V I N C I.

— The Italians are our allies.

— The brave Spanish and the Japanese too. The Japanese aren't afraid of death. They dive onto enemy targets in their planes.

The altar lights flickered at the altar boys' genuflections, at the hurried movements of the tall, pale priest. The people in the picture were only wearing nightshirts. Some were naked. But the ends of the others' nightshirts fluttered across the impure parts of their bodies. The people in the meadow began to tremble when Detlev turned round to look at the oil painting. They moved their hands, shook their heads, raised their feet. The nightshirts fluttered when the altar lights flickered. When, behind Detlev's back, the tall, pale priest shouted out the words, and Detlev stared at the picture so as not to jerk round, the painted people jumped into the air at every word, and when the little bells jingled they shook themselves like the neighbour's dog, when it came running into the summerhouse out of the rain. Sister Silissa smiled at Detlev, nodded and jerked her head several times, to make him understand that he must turn to face the altar again.

The tall, pale priest was leaning forward. The small, hoarse priest didn't wave his arms about. The tall, pale priest carried out the movements jerkily. When he raised the communion cup into the air, Detlev saw the thin arms sticking out of his lace shirt. The skin on the arms was white. Thick tufts of black hair grew out of them. Detlev's shoulders rocked back and forward. He looked back again: Three women hovered in the pale blue sky above the meadow. They carried staves and wheels and prongs which they wanted to play with. They let redcurrants fall from their hands onto the people in the meadow. The sun and the moon were painted beside the three women. The womens' bodies were swathed in fluttering clothes full of folds. They didn't tremble at the tall, pale priest's bellowing, their robes weren't blown from side to side by the wind from the watering can organ.

Once a week Detlev was allowed to walk through the church in a white surplice – from one chapel to the next – with all the other orphanage boys – singing, a stearin candle in his hand.

He didn't dare look up. He believed that in the darkness – which began beyond the radiance of the stearin candle – hovered the three women.

The stearin ran over his hand. Before it could drip down onto the ground it had cooled and congealed.

The smell rises once again. The wind, which blows across the terrace and catches the hair of the boys and girls, smells of the wet pollen in the town moat, of the fishy meadows flooded by the Salzach. Detlev imagines the smell of the stearin so strongly that he might almost have begun to look for dripping candles on the balcony.

Detlev doesn't look round. He's afraid that his movements will attract the attention of the nuns, who are now standing and waiting, not yet forcing him to interrupt his thoughts. Detlev doesn't smell the wind.

The smell of stearin grows stronger.

The hot stearin ran over his hand. Before the skin began to hurt, it lost its heat, thickened, lost its transparency, became

milky then white. Detlev liked to smell it. For a while it was
warmer than his skin. Detlev liked to feel it between his fingers, between nail and skin.

The smell reminded him of his mother, of birthday candles,
Christmas candles, of skin that had grown hot lighting candles, of fir tree needles and silver Christmas baubles covered
in stearin, of his mother's hot hair, of a single birthday candle
– his mother carried him towards it in her arms.

Finally the stearin became hard and cool. It tightened over
the skin, as the bird dropping was now tightening across the
skin. Detlev spread his fingers, clenched them into a fist.

Detlev pointed his thumb away from his forefinger. Pure
white flakes of stearin came away.

The green traces itch on the skin.

— When I'm in Hamburg I'll play with my box of building
bricks.

Detlev sees shiny limewood railings emerge between the
boys, the girls, the nuns. He imagines that, on a Friday,
when two boys are sitting in the bath tub in their linen
cloths, bright shiny buiding blocks are pushed through the
walls to destroy the wash room. He sees the boys running out
onto the church square in their wet linen cloths.

Detlev pushes the room with the bath tubs away. The windows, the cellophane panes fall inwards. The mirrors tumble
from the walls. The water slops over the edge. The bath tubs
are overturned. Their legs stick up into the air. The bath tubs
snap in two. The rust cracks loose.

Every Sunday his mother washed him again.

— It's better if I do. A mother washes her son more
thoroughly than a Catholic nun after all.

She laughed at him and called him a holy Joe when, with her,
he wanted to tie a linen cloth around himself.

— What's the cloth for?

— I don't know. But we have to have it in the orphanage, so
that the sisters don't see anything impure.

He told his mother that a mosquito had bitten him the week before. Sister Silissa had come, had lifted up his blanket, pushed up his nightshirt and rubbed ointment on the mosquito bite.
— Now confess it properly.
— What is there to confess about that? Detlev, just don't let them drive you mad.
On Monday morning Alfred asked:
— What did you do with your mother on Sunday?
— We walked to Lauterbach to visit friends from Hamburg.
— Did your mother wash you again first?
— Yes.
— How does she do that?
— You know how. You've been washed before too.
— I've forgotten. Just tell me once again.
— She undresses me and washes me.
— Completely naked?
— Yes, yes.
—That's impure. Does she kiss you as well?
— That's not impure.
— Does she scratch your back as well?
— Yes.
— A lot?
— Yes.
— And you're completely naked the whole time. That's a great sin, I have to tell you that yet again. But if you give me your bread and jam, no one else will know about your impurity.

Detlev thinks, that on the following Sunday, while his mother was washing him, he had remembered Steingriff.
— I never told mummy that.
The little wooden house in Steingriff.
Sepp took him up to the loft. The medals lay hidden beneath

the chopped wood. Sometimes they pulled the medals out
and held one against their chests.
— Who could have lost all those medals in the wood?
Detlev and Sepp weren't looking for the medals among the
faggots. They climbed over the bicycles leaning against the
lavatory wall and up to the attic, where the hay for the rabbits
was kept.
— What we're going to do now, everyone in Steingriff does.
We have to take our clothes off. It's not impure at all.
— No.
— It's called flucking.
— They sat opposite one another naked. Detlev saw that
Sepp had a mole on his hip. Detlev was shivering.
— That's not all. Next time you must bring your little bottles
from the shop with you and the pieces of plywood left over
from the fretsaw work.
— Sepp's two sisters came to fetch wood down below.
— Now we'll stick them between the beams and piss on their
heads.
The girls dropped their wood baskets, ran away. The next
time Sepp said:
— We have to stick our pipes into the little bottle and piss as
much as we can. Then we have to scratch ourselves with the
piece of wood and stick it in behind. That's what flucking
is.
On Mondays Alfred questioned Detlev. He wanted to know
what Detlev and his mother had talked about, where they
had gone, what kind of dress his mother had worn under her
coat, what they had both eaten, what Detlev had told about
the orphanage, what Detlev had thought.
Alfred remembered every word of Detlev's previous reports,
if Detlev wanted to deny something Alfred caught him out
with his own previous story, when Detlev wanted to hold
something back, Alfred guessed there was a gap every time
and drew the rest out of Detlev. Detlev became afraid of

missing out the smallest thing with Alfred. If he had done something together with his mother which he would rather have concealed from Alfred. Detlev didn't tell Alfred that he had thought of Steingriff while his mother was washing him, because he had never mentioned Steingriff. Alfred couldn't guess the name of the village. He couldn't suspect that Detlev and Sepp and the rest of the gang in the wood had found a little bag full of medals, that they hid the little bag in the chopped wood beside the lavatory and only took it out occasionally, that Detlev and Sepp had gone into the little wooden house for yet another reason, Alfred couldn't draw out of Detlev that with his mother, besides back rubbing, communion, eating cake, Hamburg, the orphanage, he had thought about the flucking in Steingriff.

Detlev forgot it again, otherwise he would have told Alfred about it without being afraid.

Detlev had only climbed up to the loft with Sepp three or four times, where the little toy bottles and the round left over pieces of plywood lay scattered in the hay, where Detlev had Sepp looked at one another, naked, and prodded one another with their fingers, with pieces of plywood, with crystal glass.

Detlev at Saint Joseph's Fountain. No one on the street. Joseph on his pedestal, black, covered in moss. Under Joseph's feet water dribbled out of a green tarnished metal pipe in the pedestal. The water collected in a stone basin. It ran out of a hole close to the rim of the basin.

— The water keeps running every day, every week, every month, every year. It was running before I was even born. It will still be running, when grandma dies, when mummy dies, when I die.

Detlev began to cry about his own death, about the death of his mother and of his grandmother.

— Perhaps we'll all die on the same day. If a bomb falls on Saint Joseph's Fountain, the water pipe will be blocked or the water will keep running out beside the fountain. Where does the water run to? Does Kriegel in the town hall have to guard the water? Does the Führer have to guard the water of all the fountains in the Greater German Reich? Is all that water not too expensive during a war?

Detlev went diagonally across the street to the shop with devotional articles: rosaries, black, white, bone coloured, brown, pink rosaries. White altar lights, red candles, black candles, pictures of saints, cellophane pictures, Marys and Josephs. The Christ Child as a baby, the Christ Child at school, the Christ Child as a man above a field, before a wood, on a lake. The Christ Child on the cross.

Detlev ran quickly away. Detlev went to the back entrance of the town hall. He remained standing by the barred windows and listened, in case a Russian, a Jew, a Pole was being whipped. He heard the clacking of a typewriter.

Detlev went down to the left to the bakery. It smelt of bakery. There was no smell of bread in the orphanage. It smelt of the Indian cattle in Hagenbeck's Zoo or it smelt like the smell Detlev imagined when he thought of the Indian cattle.

Detlev went to the front entrance of the parish church. The sacristan had locked the big door with the pointed arch. But in the big door Detlev could open a little door which was padded, like the door of his grandmother's preserves cupboard in the cellar.

The church interior was deserted, grey, with dusty coloured patches.

Detlev walked back to the town hall. He looked up at his mother's window where the geranium was in flower. The lavatory was next door.

— Mummy goes to the toilet with organ accompaniment.

— The hall for the dead gauleiter is next to it.

Detlev walked to the Lenbach Museum.

— Lenbach Street. Lenbach House. Lenbach postage stamp. Lenbach commemoration.

Detlev carried the recorder with the cleaner in a cloth case under his arm. He held the recorder book in his hand.

— The mayor, the veterinary surgeon, the parish priest eat in the Post Hotel. Artistes in town for the variety evenings eat there, as well as the new gauleiter. The wife of the general from Hamburg ate at the Market Hotel.

Detlev walked across the market place. The swing boat from the last fair was being taken down. He went to the vegetable stall, to the poultry stall, to the café by the arcade. Two signs hung in the café window: Ice Cream. Cream Cakes.

Detlev walked through the arcade tapping his recorder book against the shop windows. He went to the smithy. It smelt of singed hair, of singed wool.

His mother had leant too close to the pilot light as she was lighting the gas boiler. His mother's hair had caught fire. She extinguished the fire on her head with the bath towel. Detlev had cried because he saw his mother burning. A horse was being shod in the smithy. The horn sizzled under the hot iron. The horse didn't kick out. Detlev mounted the steps to the stationery shop. Black bound books lay in the shop window. Golden letters – like the letters on the orphanage – were impressed on the book covers.

— Large S. Small C. Small H. Small O. Double T.

The edges of the pages between the book covers were coloured red.

— Mummy's black box, in Heim Way, where cockerels' feet were boiled.

Next to the chemist's shop where his mother paid in the orphanage money – in the undertaker's room the chemist's wife had lain in front of the orphanage children with a yellow face, among flowers, amidst a smell like that of his grandmother's compost heap – Detlev looked in the window of the toy shop. German soldiers were advancing across a green mat. Some of them raised a hand grenade in the air. Two at the front held a flag. The folds in the flag looked real. Detlev clearly recognized the blood on the bandages on the heads of the hostile partisans. An Anglo–American parachutist was led away. The brave scout ventured far ahead. An enemy aircraft lay on the ground, destroyed. On the right, the general consulted a staff map. A column of soldiers marched through a burning enemy village. A brave German soldier was ambushed by a cowardly partisan. Several mobile anti-aircraft guns stood ready for action. Mortars and mine throwers were being camouflaged. A dog from a medical team was barking in front of the dressing station. It had a red tongue.

Behind the tanks, the field kitchen, the trenches, the camouflaged railway tunnels, the toy shop owner had arranged cranes made of Meccano parts, aeroplanes, biplanes, dive bombers made of perforated iron ribs, which were held together by small nuts and screws – as well as trees and people made of iron parts, an elephant and a duck.

Detlev crossed the high street and walked down the left hand side as far as the scaffolding against the Church of Our Lady. The holes in the two towers had not yet been walled up again. A week ago, prisoners of war, under guard, had brought the bells down from the towers over the scaffolding with ropes and chains. One had toppled over and shattered on the pavement. The bells were to be taken to be melted down in the munitions factory.

Detlev remembers that in front of the scaffolding he remembered the ringing of Our Lady's bells, when Sepp and Detlev and his mother came out of the wood.

Detlev walked past the convent gate to the mesh wire which separated the convent yard from the street. A large round, white circle with a fat red cross had been painted on the roof of the convent, so that enemy aircraft didn't bomb that part of the building.

From the convent windows Detlev heard the clattering of

spoons, singing, singing on the radio. On the window sills lay arms and legs like white painted building bricks or white-washed elephant's legs — pink fingers and pink toes stuck out from the white wood, the pelicans' wings on frames, wire attachments.

His mother had said:

— You're not going back to that complaining music teacher in Rosenhof any more. I don't want to say anything against him. If you meet him you must greet him politely. You can say to him – if you meet him: The paths along the Salzach are too muddy because of the flooding. He made some remarks. Who knows what he was getting at. But he's a good recorder teacher. You can say to him, if you meet him, that you're staying in a Catholic orphanage now. So you'd rather learn to play the recorder in a convent. You're a convent pupil with Mother Cecilia.

Detlev went up to the entrance. He pulled the iron handle of the bell. A man with a fat, white fist waved from above. The nun on door duty opened up. She led him up the broad stairs to the young English ladies' workrooms.

Detlev remembered the smell of Mother Cecilia, the smell of the classroom and of the plastic recorder as it grew warmer, of Mother Cecilia's recorder. It smelt of ironed aprons, of salad oil, of the paper in grandfather's desk from when he was a customs officer: Documents about the purchase of the plot of land and about paying off the mortgage on the house.

A small crucifix was hanging in the high classroom. It hung far away. Detlev couldn't make out whether the blood ran out of the wound in its side, whether the thorns pricked the forehead, whether the mouth became black, whether the fingers were bent over backwards with pain. While Mother Cecilia's outstretched index finger pointed out the notes, Detlev looked at the black wooden sections of the cross, which were trimmed with silver, on which a silver figure hung, as finely worked and glittering as Aunt Hilde's brooch, as the silver death head on the gauleiter's cap, which Detlev had also seen only as an ornament.

The smells grow weaker. The convent cloisters draw closer, so close that Detlev can see individual flagstones, which are almost too heavy to push away. Detlev shuts his eyes tightly. Detlev brushes his forehead along a pillar in the convent. He can turn his head only with an effort. The walls press in against him. Through a gap in the wall he sees Mother Cecilia passing by. Up the stairs, down the stairs. She goes round a corner and along a corridor. She steps out of a recess. She unlocks the doors.

She unlocks gates. She unlocks iron gratings. She pushes curtains aside. She takes brocade cloth out of chests. She unfolds white lace cloth. She unrolls satin. She shows him a golden goblet, set with violet and green stones. She moves golden crucifixes to the front.

— The blood is made of rubies.

She opens silver caskets.

— These are holy relics.

In the caskets lay pieces of paper with writing on them, which were tied to the bones with thread. The threads passed through holes in the bones. Mother Cecilia held up a vestment by its hanger.

— No Protestant has ever seen this before. But soon we shall take you into the Holy Catholic Church. You are going to be a priest. Perhaps one day we will consecrate you as a bishop.

Mother Cecilia threw a part of the vestment over his shoulder. Mother Cecilia held rings against his hands, against his cheeks, against his neck.

— This is emerald.

— A devotional ring.

— A ceremonial ring.

— A signet ring

— This is turmaline.
— This is a jacinth.
— This is a garnet.

Mother Cecilia's mouth no longer toot-toots into the plastic recorder to show Detlev the proper way to achieve a note. Her mouth loses the smell of socks and rhubarb. Her mouth grows as large as the main door of Our Lady's Church. Her mouth moves: Monstrance. God. God the Father. God the Son. Lacrimae. Star of the sea, I greet thee. God. Christo. Jesus. Nails. Tongs. Chalcedony. The words hook into the eyes which link the bloody tears of the saints to one another. Mother Cecilia fades into the flames. She is borne aloft like the black paper of the seed packets, the shreds of the kite, above the autumn fires in the allotments. Mother Cecilia falls to the ground, lies there like the half burned teddy bear that grandfather had thrown out. Detlev throws it away. He pulls off the roof with the round white disc and the red cross. He pulls apart the steel and wire frames. He sweeps the plaster into a hole. He piles the pointed sacristy windows one on top of the other. He takes the hay and the plywood remnants from the loft. Detlev knocks down the little wooden house. On the balcony the fluttering of eyelashes, the twitching of pupils, the expanding of ribs as breathing grows slower. The short threads of the bird dropping are torn between Detlev's fingers. The orphanage children, the nuns, Detlev remain fixed, like lead before it melts.

— They've really all gone now. The oatmeal cake is gone. The convent of the young English ladies is gone. Steingriff too.

This time he wasn't walking alone. He was walking with Anna. He was wearing his brightly coloured Bavarian jacket. They were walking along a country road lined by hop poles. Women were picking the hop flowers.

Earlier Detlev and Anna had travelled by train. His mother didn't know anything about it.

— Detlev's mother is afraid.

Detlev doesn't know why he and Anna had been sent to Aichach.

— Sister Silissa thinks that it's better if I don't say.

— A white lie, that's allowed occasionally. That won't hurt your mother. Quite the opposite, you're reassuring her. Otherwise she would only get upset.

— Why does Detlev's mother get upset easily?

The country road had been mended with tar and gravel. Detlev picked up a little piece of gravel. Anna knocked it out of his hand. It fell onto the green cuff of his jacket.

— Your soul receives a mark like that for every sin that you commit.

Detlev was afraid in the dark. When he was alone in the dark. When his mother had left him alone or when he woke up and the others were sleeping. The jumping jacks grew giant noses. The teddy bear's eyes swelled out of its head.

Detlev was afraid on the way to Mrs Weindeln's house. He wasn't alone. The sun was in the middle of the sky. The light fell vertically onto the road, the fields, the hop poles, the women, the children.

Anna held her head to the side and looked up.

Her eyelids fluttered rapidly up and down

The sun shone so brightly, that the landscape and the people in it appeared withered and shrunken to Detlev. The sunlight hung between him and the people like thick glass, like sewing machine oil.

Everything was distanced, detached. Anna too. She stiffened in the light, like a figure in the picture with the three hovering women.

Detlev looked towards the horizon, yellow in the distance above the grey painted meadows. Detlev remembered the meadows rising and falling into the distance. He was afraid that the naked dead could climb out of the roadsides ditches, or that the three women with hands full of redcurrants could come swishing past under the sun. He said:

— I'm not afraid.

— What are you saying?

Detlev held onto the front of his trousers with fear.

— Detlev, don't touch yourself like that. That's impure. If the sisters knew that. Sister Silissa put Erwin across her knee only the day before yesterday because he's always touching himself there.

— I have to pee.

— Wait till we're at Mrs Weindeln's house. The hop pickers might see you.

— Who is Mrs Weindeln?

— A holy woman.

— Why are we going there?

Detlev's mind skips over the answer. His mind rests only on the next question, which he hears once again.

— Why is Mrs Weindeln holy?

— She's holy.

Detlev hears the question from nine months before a second time.

— Why is Mrs Weindeln holy?

— Don't you believe that she's holy?

— I believe it. But I want to know why.

— One must have proper faith. You're just a Protestant after all.

Anna stopped. She held her head to the side and looked up again and blinked. She was silent. Detlev didn't dare to take her by the hand or say anything to her.

The sun shone down so brightly on the landscape, that the grass appeared yellow and the asphalt white. Still holding her head to the side, Anna looked past Detlev.

— Perhaps invisible angels are drawing her soul out now? Perhaps she's turning into a pillar of salt, as it says in the Bible?

Anna walked beside him

— Mrs Weindeln is holy because in the street in front of her house she found a leaf with the Lord Jesus Christ on it. It was a leaf from a pear tree. It was half rotted away. The Lord Jesus Christ looked at Mrs Weindeln from the dirty lead as if he had been crocheted. Damn, don't tell them at the orphanage that I said dirty leaf and Lord Jesus Christ in one breath.

— No.

— Swear it by the Holy Sacraments.

— I swear.

— Your swearing is no use at all. You don't receive the sacraments. Anyway with a Protestant one never knows if he's not drawing off the oath with his other hand again.

— I want to become a Catholic.

— Then perhaps your swearing counts half and half. If you bear false witness, you'll go to hell.

— I'm not bearing false witness.

— But you can't become a Catholic.

— Why not?

— Because of original sin.

— What's that?

Anna didn't know. Detlev knows now – after having repeated to himself this part of the conversation from the trip to Aichach every evening for nine months.

— Anna doesn't know anything.

— You can only become a Catholic if you're something very special – if you're at least as holy as Mrs Weindeln.

— How do I become holy?

— You have to find a leaf with the Lord Jesus Christ on it.

— Anyway Mrs Weindeln didn't find it at all, it was the sacristan in Schrobenhausen.

— You think you know it all.

— I want to become holy because of something else. Perhaps there aren't so many leaves with the Lord Jesus Christ on them. What else is holy about Mrs Weindeln?

— She prays all day long – even when she's cooking and eating and drinking and when she's doing something unclean. Of course she never does anything that's impure. She has lots of litres of holy water and many consecrated, black storm candles. She castigates herself bitterly.

— What does castigate oneself bitterly mean?

— So that in the hour of her death she will ascend in the flesh directly to heaven.

— Is there no other way in which I can become a Catholic?

— You would have to carry a thirty foot cross all round the town wall for three days. But you're too weak to do that.

Detlev knows he's too weak, he's too weak for a thirty foot cross, like the ones on the enamel reliefs on Calvary Hill, under which the Lord Jesus Christ, God's son, God's only begotten son, the Saviour, the Redeemer, the Prince of Peace, the Christ Child – almost collapsing – his face raised – is making his way.

— I'm too weak to do that. Even Alfred is too weak to do it, or Odel, or Joachim-Devil. It takes four of the big ones to carry the soup pot into the dining room.

Detlev picks up the leaves under the peach tree. They're small and they all have leaf curl. Detlev collects leaves from the cinder path by the quince tree, on the slope by the birch. He holds them up against the clouds. The leaves are full of holes, black and yellow, wet. He looks to see whether the larger and smaller ribs, the decaying remains don't form two ears, a nose, a mouth, two raised fingers, a wound on the back of the hand, thorns, blood.

— Do you think the Holy Passion hurt a lot?

— Quite a lot. I don't really know. It's so long ago.

On the enamel relief Jesus is wearing a pink shirt. He turns his eyes towards heaven. His father looks out from behind a cloud. Judas is wearing a green shirt. His lips are black. They are stuck fast to the face of Lord Jesus Christ. Judas's lips look like the snout of a wild pig in the zoo. The apostles all have beards. Peter draws his sword. The men-at-arms wear the armour from the Lenbach Museum.

— The Passion must have hurt the Lord Jesus Christ a lot. But he knew that he would soon be with his Father in heaven again, while Judas is already hanging on the tree and the devils are hammering nails through every little corner of his soul. All betrayers go to hell. You too, Detlev, if you betray anything of our conversation and that I said dirty leaf and Lord Jesus Christ in one breath.

— But Anna, they whipped him, and with spikes on the thongs, just as Kriegel does. They pressed rose stems with very long thorns onto his head. Just imagine it. This moment. Imagine they were doing it to you here. Your skin would be torn, and the thorns would pierce your bones and enter your head.

— That's nothing at all. You can't possibly know everything that the Lord Jesus Christ had to suffer for our sins. They called him King of the Jews. They shouted: It serves the Jewish dog, the Jewish swine right. They pulled out finger nails, thrust him under water, crushed his feet. They bound him to an electric-shock machine.

— All that hurt. Would you like them to hurt you? So that as a reward you'll be allowed to sit beside God's throne afterwards.

— That is blasphemous pride. Don't be sinful.

The hop poles had come to an end. The road passed through the meadows in broad curves. Detlev and Anna's heels, soles, pattered on the white asphalt. They followed the winding road. Bushes with limp leaves hid Detlev at the bends in the road. They didn't talk any more. They ran down the steep slope. They didn't laugh as they ran. Anna took Detlev's hand. Detlev felt that her hand was warmer than his. Her head was far away behind the glass pane of an oil painting. She held her head to the side and looked up again. She resembled a nymph or a priestess on the picture of the

festival behind the armchair in which his grandmother had
her afternoon nap.

Detlev imagined the holy woman's house, which he would
soon see. He saw her dressed in a sack sitting underneath a
gaping straw roof. Her legs were thin. Her arms and her neck
were thin. He saw her in an allotment hut beneath dangling
roof board.

Anna walked more slowly. Detlev looked down. He saw
Anna's knee socks, in turn, in step.

Detlev dared to look down. The conversation about the Passion had overcome his fear of the bones which might stick up
out of the road.

— It's broad daylight. There are two of us.

Anna cried:

— Hazel nuts.

She let go of Detlev's hand. She ran up a hill. She grew
smaller as she ran, and the sound of her movements was
lost in the distance. At the top the hazel bushes hung over
the edge of the hill. Anna knelt down among the branches.
She smoothed down her dress.

— Now you're one of the three hovering women with the
little toy hammers on the picture in the church. You have
a blue dress. They have a red dress.

— There's no picture with dresses in the church.

— Yes there is, in the parish church.

— I haven't seen it. Eat some hazel nuts. You have to bite
them open with your teeth.

Anna cracked three hazel nuts. She held out to him the splin-
tered shells full of saliva and the furry brown kernels.

— They're just ripe. Take some home and plant them. In
a few months you can harvest hazel nuts in front of the
orphanage.

— I don't know if I'm going to stay long in the orphanage.

— You'll stay. We've all been there for a long time. No one
gets away again so quickly. Only if there's something out of

the ordinary about you. If there's something wrong with you. If you act dirtily and behave indecently, then the people from the Party take you away. If you like eating hazel nuts, take some with you and plant them. You'll see.

— It hurt most, when he was hanging on the cross. His whole body hung by two nails through his hands. It must have taken a long time, until he died. Two nails through the hands are very painful. But no one dies from that.

— They had hammered a nail through his feet as well. That nail helped to support the body and increased the loss of blood. Eat the nuts, don't say any more, Detlev. You only need to look at the crucifix in the dining room. A little block is stuck under his feet. That must have held him up. And he was already exhausted beforehand. So the loss of blood from his hands and his feet was enough to cause death. Perhaps our dear Lord allowed the end to come a little faster with his son. Eat nuts, come over here right into the middle of the bushes.

— My father is far away. I don't know where he is. I would accept that they hurt me, until I died, if in return I could sit beside our heavenly Father in heaven.

— Don't blaspheme. I've already told you that once. Pray properly. Confess properly. No, you're not allowed to confess. Probably they have to flay you in purgatory first, before you can enter through Heaven's Gate.

— Perhaps he died because they struck him in the heart?

— No, when they stabbed him through the heart, stagnant water flowed out and clots of blood. He had already been dead for a long time. The curtain in the temple was already torn and the dead were climbing out of their graves. They only stabbed him through the heart to find out if he was dead.

Over the hollow in the meadow from which naked men and women were clambering, hovered the three women, holding little toy hammers and iron bars in front of them.

Redcurrants fell out of their hands beside the iron tools.
The stagnant air beneath the leaves, the green light became
thicker and heavier. The oil for the sewing machine or the
glass cube, through which he spoke to Anna, cut him off
completely. He saw himself like a black ant with outstretched
legs – with one severed leg from the martyrdom thousands of
years before
— The amber is thousands of years old.
in a polygon of amber on his mother's necklace.
— Anna, who are the three women in red hovering over the
meadows in the picture in the church?
— It's a martyrdom. They're holding out the instruments
of their martyrdom. That's not a little toy hammer. Their
clothes are red from the blood of a thousand wounds. The
blood drips from their hands onto the vision. Nothing was
spared them.
— I'm afraid again. In a moment the ground here is going to
start quaking again. The sun will fall down to earth and there
will be a deep fissure in the road.
— Be still. Don't shout it out. Come in here under the
leaves. They crawled deeper into the spreading bushes.
Detlev jammed his head between his knees.
Detlev said:
— Can he hear us?
— He always hears us.
— Can you feel the ground quaking yet?
— Pray for it not to quake.
— Is he there, wherever we are?
— Probably. I don't know. If he can hear us.
— If he can hear us, he must be there.
— You can't see him. Don't talk about it any more.
Otherwise he'll punish us. We're quite alone here. Apart
from Him. No one's walking along the road. Perhaps he's
walking along the road right now and we can't see him.
— He can hear you. He's standing behind you, Anna.

— I'll run away. I'll leave you sitting here.
She didn't stand up. She didn't move. The leaves of the hazel
bush scratched their ears and hands. The dip in the meadow,
the empty road shimmered through the foliage.
— You can run away. I'm staying. I'm not frightened any
more. He is everywhere. I want to become a saint. He can
hear it now. If you don't want to become a saint he'll pick
you up and fly high in the air with you and let you fall from
his claws and you'll be pierced by a sharp rock.
Anna parted the bushes. The twigs caught her dress. She
screamed:
— The devil is coming.
She ran down the hill towards the road. She stopped just
before the road. Detlev caught up with her. She held her
head to the side and looked up. She tried to bite herself in
the hand. She fell down. She lashed out with her arms. A
green, black and grey speckled lorry drove past. It had a
camouflaged trailer. It drove slowly. The engine hammered
and squealed.
Anna stood up again.
— I was so frightened of the thundering lorry. It was coming
from the munitions factory and was heavily loaded. Don't
tell anyone that you've seen the lorry. Don't tell that I said
there's a munitions factory. Otherwise we'll be taken away
and executed.
Anna walked slowly. She was tired.
Detlev doesn't remember holy Mrs Weindeln. He remembers a rusty bicycle, a water pump, a pot with green soap,
a large brush.
Mrs Weindeln helped him remove the spots of tar from his
jacket.
The coffin stood in front of the altar. When the orphanage
children pushed along the benches, the coffin was not far
from the first bench – between the first two pillars of the
nave, in front of the first altar step.

It wasn't a coffin. It was a block, as tall as Detlev. Over the block, over the wooden frame, over the cardboard casing a black cloth had been laid. At the corners the folds had been smoothed out and pinned to the altar carpet. The moulding, the bevelling of a coffin were visible under the black cloth.

Detlev no longer knows whether a sword, a knight's cross, a bunch of gentians, bunch of roses lay on the black cloth.

Detlev no longer knows where the people in black sat. They sat on an extra bench in front of the coffin, or they sat in the gallery or on the right or on the left in front of the altar or on extra chairs between the benches for the girls and the benches for the boys.

The parish priest was dressed differently from usual. He wore a black, silver embroidered chasuble. The parish priest wore the black, silver embroidered chasuble each time that the extra bench with four or five or six or seven black veiled people stood there, when the block with the black cloth was set up in front of it and the sword and the cap, edelweiss, the bunch of gentians, the roses, the Knight's Cross, the Iron Cross first or second class lay on it.

At a certain point during the mass there was shooting outside.

— What's that?

— That's the gun salute.

— Where does that happen?

— At the town wall.

— How does the man at the cannon know when to shoot?

Alfred shrugged his shoulders. Detlev thought of the sacristan. The sacristan ran out of mass and up the church tower with a white flag and waved across to the wall. Then the shot was fired.

Or someone who was standing by the altar signalled to the main door. At the main door someone signalled to the town hall. At the town hall someone signalled to the hotel. Someone from the hotel to the chemist. The chemist passed on the signal to the wall.

— A fallen soldier has earned it.

The faces of the members of the family could not be made out under their veils.

The face of the widow and the face of the mother of the fallen soldier could not be made out under the black veils.

Against the black cloth the white handkerchiefs looked like broken egg shells which his grandfather mixed with the soft boiled potatoes for the hens.

— It's good, because then the hens will lay beautiful new eggs again.

His grandmother said:

— It's not good. The hens only get used to eating the egg shells. Then afterwards they only eat their own eggs.

The father, the uncle, the sons were wearing black suits. The widow, the sisters, the daughters wept under black veils. The boys didn't weep.

— The boys are brave.

— Is the fallen soldier under the cloth?

— It's a mass for the dead in absentia.

Detlev had believed that the soldier was lying under the cloth, because the widow was weeping and because the parish priest sprinkled holy water on the cloth, on the helmet and the bunch of flowers and the sword, because the organ played and the gun salute was fired.

— The fallen are broken in pieces.

Detlev had believed that after the battle the captain walked across the field looking for the dead and wounded. The dead were put in coffins and, accompanied by sad music, transported home on a carriage drawn by black horses.

— Sometimes all that is left of the brave soldiers who have fallen is a little bit of skin and hair and a button and their service pouch.

Detlev thought that everything – the hands black with blood, the shattered head, the broken limbs – the torn-off head, the broken forehead, the eyes lay next to one another in the coffin under the cloth.

— It's not a coffin. It's a dummy.

Detlev thought:

— I would only need to go up to it and lift the cloth and push the coffin lid aside, then the fallen soldier will be lying there and everyone can see him, like the gauleiter in the town hall.

Detlev wanted to know what the dead look like all over their bodies. Detlev wanted to know what the head of a dead person looks like and what the skin and the intestines in the stomach look like. He wanted to know whether it's true that soldiers are torn in two parts or in four, and that the captain and the medical orderlies sometimes don't find all the parts again.

It was only a dummy.

The widow, the mother, the daughters had black cloths over their faces. A black cloth lay over the dummy.

Detlev is frightened of finding bones from an earlier war in the ditch between Lokstedt and Eimsbüttel.

The widow, the mother, the daughters wept, as if the dead soldier was lying before them, as if the captain had really collected the pieces and sent them home – not just the cap or the helmet or the sword.

The soldier wasn't in the church. The soldier no longer lay whole on the field. The soldier was dead. The soldier was gone. The dead soldier was nowhere to be found.

Anna on the balcony. The strokes of her pigtails on either side of her face.

Anna didn't run after him on the balcony. Anna spoke to Detlev in the washroom, where linen cloths hung over the rims of the bath tubs.

— Is there something you should tell me, Detlev?

— Is there something you should tell me?

— Did you blabber something to Alfred about the trip to Aichach?

— Not me. And you?

— I didn't either – not to Alfred.

— Who to then?

— Joachim-Devil asked me whether I had committed a sin on the trip to Aichach.

Not me, I told Joachim-Devil. And Detlev? he asked.

— He didn't either, I said.

What did Detlev do then, if he didn't commit a sin?

Detlev said that his father is just as far away as the father of Lord Jesus Christ. He touched himself at the front of his trousers as he was walking. He doubted the holiness of Mrs Weindeln a little.

That's not so bad at all, said Joachim-Devil. Just tell me a little bit more about the trip to Aichach and especially about Detlev. — I really didn't want to tell any more. But then Alfred said: What you're telling us about Detlev is very funny. It makes us laugh. Detlev is a clever boy. — I had to laugh myself, and I said: Detlev said, that if one keeps very still during torment, then one will be allowed to sit beside the Lord God afterwards. — Really, Detlev will become a saint or at least a parish priest. Tell us more. — Detlev told me about the dress in church. He said: You are a saint too, Anna. — Now we know everything, Anna. Now you shall learn the truth. You have been chosen by Providence to avert many mortal sins. Perhaps with your help we will even manage to save Detlev. Detlev is on the path of heresy. At first we pretended that it wasn't so bad, to keep you talking without any fear. Detlev is lost if he goes on like this. He must be deterred, otherwise the Lord Jesus will let him fall, and he will remain in hell for all eternity. We want to pretend to be the devil one night, so that Detlev sees what he can expect. — I betrayed you Detlev. First

I listened to your heretical talk, then I betrayed you, and now I'm betraying again by telling you what Alfred and Joachim-Devil intend to do to you. I am a betrayer. I shall go to hell. I didn't know my father and my mother. When I get upset, I go into convulsions, and if they hadn't taken me into the orphanage, I would have been buried long ago. I shall go to hell. As long as I live, the Host of the Holy Communion will strengthen and nourish me, so that when I die, I shall descend to hell all fat and plump and there will be plenty of flesh on me, which the devils can cut from me.

Those were mortal sins that we committed on the way to Aichach. We shall never make that good. Detlev interrupted Anna once during the five minutes that she talked:

— Don't stare so wildly. Otherwise you'll have your convulsions again. I didn't have any evil thoughts on the trip to Aichach. Whatever did I do?

— And I did nothing? I cursed the Holy Name. I said dirty leaf and Lord Jesus Christ in the same breath. You didn't betray me. I betrayed you, in order to wash myself clean of the anathema. In the hour of my death I shall enter a second hell because I betrayed you. For you there will perhaps be deliverance. Also you're a Protestant, so it all doesn't weigh so heavily. You're not so great a sinner as I. I am afraid. But you shouldn't be afraid. Alfred and Joachim-Devil want to make the devil appear to you. They say, to keep you out of everlasting hell – in reality only to torment you for fun. No one can save the likes of us from hell. The holy sisters can't do it, the parish priest can't. Perhaps not even holy Mrs Weindeln. If anyone can, then only the Pope. Joachim-Devil is going to imitate the voice of the real devil. That should suit him. They're going to beat on the door and say the devil is nailing together the planks for your coffin. Don't believe it. Remain silent. They're going to talk through combs wrapped in cellophane.

Anna advised him to pretend not to know anything. Anna didn't know her brothers, or her sisters nor her father and her mother. By her betrayal Anna wanted to wash herself clean of the anathema from Aichach.

In order to wash herself clean of the betrayal, she betrayed the plans of Alfred and Joachim-Devil to Detlev. She was afraid of no longer being able to wash herself clean of her sins at all, she was afraid of only dyeing her soul blacker and blacker, like white linen cloths which instead of becoming whiter in the wash only became blacker from being immersed in the water. Perhaps later she would have to go from one hell to the next, as she had been sent from one institution to the next, to escape death, to discharge her sins in all eternity, she said.

Alfred, Odel, Joachim-Devil in the group in front of Detlev on the balcony.

— Joachim-Devil is called Joachim-Devil because through his wickedness he doesn't get plump. He looks like the devil incarnate under the feet of the Virgin Mary on the cellophane picture 'Star of the Sea I greet thee'. Joachim-Devil wasn't big and strong. He ran back and forward between the big strong boys. He never hit Detlev. He didn't hit anyone else either. He was frightened of being hit. If one of the boys was cross with him, Joachim-Devil looked for someone else to protect him. He watched when the big strong boys had a fight or when they all set upon one boy. He was quicker than the others. He eavesdropped. He passed on what he had heard. Everyone was repelled by him. The big strong boys were afraid of him. He was seldom hit. No one would have accepted a present from him. The nuns pinched his ears. They didn't give him any sweets.

Odel was stupid. He ran after the others. Not out of fear like Joachim-Devil, but because he didn't know what to do if left to himself. He didn't tell tales. He just ran slowly from one to another. He never defended himself. No one attacked him.

He was fat. He had red hair. He wet his bed. He wasn't laughed at because of it. He would not have been angry if he had been laughed at. Once he had a tantrum. Odel grabbed the nearest boy and struck him in the face with a tin plate, so that blood dripped onto his shoes.

The nun said:

— You're all to blame. Odel is good-natured. Odel doesn't harm anyone. Why did you have to go too far in provoking him?

For a whole year Odel and Detlev went to school side by side.

Detlev remembers waking up. The air around him was like black glass. He heard the breathing of the others. It sounded as if gigantic thin men were approaching the bed on every side and the glass cracked at each of their steps. Detlev remembers the fear he felt beside Anna in the midday sunshine between the hop poles.

The white moon was sticking to the black church tower. The moon was made of cardboard, the church tower too. The moon shone on the cobblestones. Detlev looked at the church tower. The glass around Detlev grew paler. The church tower became four cornered. The moon turned into heavy black masonry. The moon became more distant than Aichach or Munich. The sky began far beyond the moon. The air between the sky and the moon and the church tower and Detlev's bed didn't move. Detlev held his breath. He didn't turn his neck. He wanted to listen carefully, in case anyone was coming closer behind the walls or behind the moon.

Detlev breathed regularly again.

— Otherwise the others will notice that I've woken up.

He didn't swallow his saliva. He opened his eyes so wide that, whatever happened, he would have been able to recognize a large shadow or many large eyes in the dormitory. He tried hard not to let his eyelashes quiver.

Detlev heard:
— Are you both ready? I'm ready.
Odel? A dead man? A sister? A devil? Odel. Detlev saw Odel's lips before him – the drops of spittle as his lips moved. The teeth behind the lips. Sometimes the spittle formed a bubble as he was speaking. He spoke slowly. The bubble burst again.
Afred said:
— Me too.
Joachim-Devil said:
— Me too.
— Let's start.
Detlev heard Odel climb out of his bed, go to the washroom door, raise one of his slippers and strike the door with it. Detlev heard the rubber sole of the slipper strike the wood. Odel struck regularly. He counted: — One, two – and struck. Odel wanted to strike with the same force each time. Sometimes the blow was uneven and Detlev heard first the edge of the sole strike the wood and immediately afterwards the felt of the slipper; sometimes Odel struck the door frame and it gave off a different sound from when he struck the border of the ornamentation in the middle.
Detlev felt himself jump with fright. A vein under his chin throbbed up and down. With each new blow of the slipper the saliva pushed Detlev's tongue higher. Odel waited. He didn't strike the door any more.
— Now it's over. Odel didn't strike the door with his slipper at all. It was a door banging shut. A piece of tin from the gutter knocking against the wall. No one said: Let's start. I was dreaming. Someone was talking in his dream. I must go to sleep again. It's still a long time till morning. I'll sleep right through. I won't see Sister Silissa when she comes in to make her round and turn the pages in the prayer book.
Sister Silissa didn't come. Detlev didn't fall asleep. He heard the others swallow their saliva, carefully push their hands down under the blanket.

The walls sank down. The windows, the doors flew away. Moonlight speckled their faces. The moonlight was reflected in their eyes. Detlev closed his eyes. Detlev heard Odel go back to his bed and pull out the chamber pot, which was still empty, which rang as it was dragged across the floor, and call into it:
— Detlev.
Odel went to the washroom door with the chamber pot. Joachim-Devil didn't have a chamber pot under his bed. In a high voice he squeaked:
— Detlev.
Alfred cried into his cupped hands:
— Detlev.
Then the three didn't cry out any more.
Detlev swallowed the saliva. He couldn't gulp down all the saliva in one go. He opened his mouth. He coughed and spat out the saliva in long strings over the bed.
— Now I've moved. Now they've heard me coughing. Now they'll jump onto my bed.
In Hamburg they lay under the bed too. His mother sat on the edge of Detlev's bed. Beside her feet in the dark, to the right and to the left, they looked out. Detlev saw their noses, their eyes, their legs.
Detlev saw Alfred's nose. It swelled up. It grew as large as the rest of his body. It gleamed violet in the moonlight. Thick tufts of hair grew in the nostrils. When Alfred breathed, the tufts began to rattle and clatter and blood dripped down instead of snot. The veins lay on the surface of the nose, one vein next to the other, thick as garden hoses.
Detlev saw Odel's face before him. Odel's nose disappeared. The eyes swelled out. Foam appeared at the edges of his eyes with the strain. The eyes grew large as plates. Skin flaked from Odel's eyes like enamel. Instead of the black tin of a plate lumps of red flesh appeared. Thick drops of blood ran over the bulging eyes into Odel's noseless face.

Detlev saw Joachim's back. Joachim had a black tail, under the tail a large, black hole. The hole widened until it occupied half his back. Blood flowed out of it.

In Hamburg when his mother said the prayer about the many angels, the big noses, the countless giant fingers jostled up against his mother's feet.

— Two to my right, two to my left, two at my head, two, two, two. . .

Detlev didn't cough any more. He rubbed his fingers together – as he did now with the bird dropping.

Odel struck the washroom door again with his slipper.

— Detlev, we are the three devils. And one devil is hammering the nails into your coffin, said all three at once. Odel into the chamber pot. Alfred into his hands, Joachim-Devil in a squeaky voice.

They spoke loudly and slowly. The words got mixed up. Joachim-Devil started before Alfred and Odel. Odel hadn't finished the first word, when Alfred and Joachim-Devil were already saying the next one.

Alfred whispered:

— This isn't they way to do it. He won't believe us. We have to do it differently.

— One of us says it quietly first of all. The others repeat it loudly.

— Now wailing and moaning and chattering teeth first! Have you got the paper and the combs?

They wrapped cellophane round the combs, as Anna had said they would, and held the combs and paper to their lips.

— Oh, oh, said Joachim-Devil quietly.

— Oh, oh, cried all three together.

Detlev thinks:

— Oh, oh, the cat's got an ache, the dog's in a rage. He'll no' go to school for an age. – The cat, the dog.

— We're suffering.

— We're suffering, we're suffering, we're suffering, we're suffering.

— And now we're here because of you.

— And now we're here because of you.

— Because every Sunday evening you let yourself be washed, naked, by your mother.

— Because every Sundayeveningevening, Sundayevening-evening you let yourself be washed naked.

— Because you drew the Christ Child with something impure between his legs.

— Because you painted the Christ Child – in a drawing, in the drawing pad, on a sheet of paper – between the legs – painted him with something impure between his legs.

Detlev coughed. He sat up, coughing. Saliva and sweat soaked his nightshirt, the sheet.

— That's not true, it wasn't anything impure. It was only the Christ Child's leg. I drew the Christ Child running.

— I saw it myself. It was impure.

— Alfred is right. I saw it.

— We are the three devils, sent by the eternal council. We are to fetch you.

— Knock, Odel.

— Knock, Odel.

— Do you believe that we are the three devils?

— Do you believe that we are the three devils?

— Yes.

Odel struck the washroom door.

— On the trip to Aichach you touched your impure place and wanted to show it to Anna.

— On the trip to Aichach you touched your impure place and wanted to show it to Anna.

— You wanted to lead Anna away from the true Catholic path. You promised her money and sausages and cakes.

— You wanted to lead Anna away from the true Catholic path. You promised her sausages and cakes and sausages and medals and money and cakes and sausages and cakes and medals.

— You said: I myself am a Christ Child. You said: My mother is the Virgin Mary. You said: My father is the dear Lord Jesus Christ.

— You said: I myself am the Christ Child. – Jesus Christ in the crib – on the cross.

My mother is the Virgin Mary. You said: My mother is the Virgin Mary. You said: My father is God in heaven. You said: Our Father in heaven. You said: My father is God the Father. You said:

— That is blasphemous pride. And even if you were him, what has happened to the flight to Egypt? Just because your father is dead. Because the Lord Jesus Christ – our beloved infant Jesus was not without a father at all. He has two fathers. Saint Joseph and our Father in Heaven.

— And that's why we're hammering the nails into your coffin.

— And that's why we're hammering the nails into your coffin.

— It'll be ready right away.

— It'll be ready right away.

— These are the final blows.

— These are the final blows.

Sweat ran into Detlev's eyes. The flickering wings, the twinkling tails, the cracking noses, the exploding eyes pressed against his retina between eye and lid. Detlev opened his eyes wide. The dormitory was black.

— We're going to fly to you now with the coffin and put you in it.

— We're going to fly to you now with the coffin and put you into it.

— We're coming.

— We're coming. We're coming. We're coming. We're coming.

— Mummy. Mummy. Mummy. Mummy. Mummy.
Mummy.

As the rustling of the cellophane increased, as Odel struck the
washroom door more quickly, as Alfred and Joachim-Devil
threw their combs on the floor, Detlev could no longer
scream out the whole word. Only the ee was left. He
screamed ee, till the air gave out and the saliva suffocated
the last syllable.

— Are you going to be humble from now on? Then it will be
all right again.

— We have to be quick, otherwise Sister Silissa will be here,
Odel, Alfred.

— Are you going to be humble from now on? Then it will be
all right again. We have to be quick, otherwise Sister Silissa
will be here, Odel, Alfred.

Joachim-Devil said:

— You're stupid, Odel, Alfred. Odel, Alfred, wake up. I am
the devil. There are three devils here. You listen too, Odel,
Alfred and you as well Joachim, while Detlev swears. Swear,
Detlev.

— I want to be humble. I want to be humble.

— Did you hear Joachim, Odel, Alfed, what Detlev has
sworn. I am the devil. Answer, now.

Alfred said:

— Odel, Joachim-Devil, did you hear, the devils are here and
want to fetch Detlev.

Detlev heard Odel and Joachim-Devil yawning.

Odel said:

— Joachim-Devil, Alfred says the three proper devils are
here and want to fetch Detlev.

Joachim-Devil said:

— Well, why don't you drive them away? We've got to
help poor Detlev. The sign of the Holy Cross is enough,
after all. And if that doesn't work, then we'll just have to
fetch Sister Silissa and say that the three devils are here

because of Detlev's sins, and that we can't get rid of them
alone.

In the name of the Father –

— The name of the Father. What is the name of the Father?

— and of the Son and of the Holy Ghost. They're gone, we
don't need to tell Sister Silissa anything at all. You'd prefer
that, wouldn't you, Detlev?

— Yes.

— It was sufficient for them to pronounce the name of the
Father. The name of the Father is very powerful – if they
were three proper devils. If they weren't three proper devils,
I don't know how powerful the name of the Father is. The
name is powerful. Otherwise Sister Silissa wouldn't pray.
Otherwise Frieda wouldn't have promised me the prayer of
conversion. Otherwise there wouldn't be a Catholic Church.
Otherwise I wouldn't need to pray, in order to be turned into
a Catholic.

Alfred said:

— You cried for your mother.

— How do you know that?

— I heard it while I was half asleep. Your mother doesn't
care about you. Perhaps your mother would rather that you
were dead. If we had a mother, she would have protected us
from the devils. Three devils can't do anything at all against a
proper Catholic mother even if they did have prickly, forked
tails and bodies all covered in thick black hairs. We protected
you. You have us to thank for that.

Detlev remembers:

The letters were printed on white sheets. A whole row of
small U's, a row of small E's, a row of small I's. The card
was lightly punched between the rows, so that the rows with
the small I and the small K and the large K and small P could

be cleanly torn off. He had to cut out each I and Qu and R and S separately with the scissors.

— You're not cutting them out carefully and neatly. Evenly and neatly like all the other boys.

A little red cellophane picture lay flat beside the sheets of letters. The Virgin Mary hovered on a narrow sickle moon above a sea of tall waves. A thin crooked devil with pointed horns and a long forked tail was wriggling along the sickle moon.

'Star of the sea I greet thee,' it said on the first line below the sea. On the next line was:

'O Mary, come to our aid.'

— Because you're a Protestant and despite that pay close attention in the Catholic religion lesson.

The small, hoarse priest had a box full of different coloured cellophane pictures.

The detached and cut out letters were squeezed into the compartments of the letter case. The large A's by themselves. The small A's by themselves. The large B's by themselves. The small B's by themselves. When he shouldered his satchel, swung it back and forward, ran, the letter case bounced up and down, the letters fell out and got mixed up. Then Detlev picked them from the frayed leather bottom of the satchel, between the chalk pencils and the pencil case with the painted ducks and the little exercise book with pen wipers and the reading book, the best writing book, the pen box.

He had to arrange the letters once again and fit the individual piles into the letter case again. 'Our Führer was a mason,' it said on one little cellophane picture. The Führer was printed on the cellophane picture in yellowish outline. The Führer gazed up at a half-finished house. Beams stuck into the air. No windows gleamed in the window cavities. A garland with fluttering ribbons hung on the roof frame. Flags billowed behind the Führer. The Führer bent down to a schoolboy.

Detlev laid the little blue and red cellophane pictures on top of the undetached and uncut sheets of letters. The rows of letters could be made out through the tinted cellophane. The outlines of the Führer, of the house, of the Virgin Mary lay on top of the small I, the large B, the small B, the small Sh. The yellow lines of the drawings and the yellow letters of the captions 'Star of the sea I greet thee, oh Mary, come to our aid' and 'Our Führer was a mason' hid individual black letters on the sheets beneath.

— Your ears are as large as Jew ears, but you work hard, you have an Aryan expression on your face, and your hair is blonde.

Detlev breathed on the little blue cellophane picture. The Führer's arm reached upwards. The beams of the house bent. The cellophane picture curled up like the roofing board in the potato fire. Detlev blew the Führer and the house and the flags and the schoolboy back and forward across the sheets of letters.

Detlev breathed on the red cellophane picture, blew till it rolled. One after the other the two little pictures became straight and flat again.

The pale priest had shouted at Detlev during the religion lesson, because Detlev hadn't raised his arm high enough for the sign of the cross. One of the boys in the class helped Detlev:

— Detlev is a Protestant.

Detlev opened the letter case. Some compartments were empty. Detlev detached rows of letters and cut off the individual letters. He fitted a large S, a small T, a small A, a small R, a small O, a small F, then a small T, a small H, a small E, a large S, another small E, then a small A between the moulding on the lid of the letter case. He scratched the words away again with his nails.

'The devil,' he put on the first line.

'Alfred is a devil,' he placed on the line below.

'Odel' – he scratched the word away again.

'Otto is a devil too.'

Below that:

'Joachim-Devil is also a –'

Below that:

'Devil'

The small E's and the small L's were used up. Detlev didn't cut off any more. He scratched till the lid was empty again. On the middle line he put:

'Our dear God.'

He took away the third word and the full stop again. He put the word together again. Pushed the full stop behind it again. Onto the line below he once more pushed a large G, a small O, a D.

Detlev tried to remember what the word 'God' had sounded like, before he had put it together on the lid of the letter case. He repeated the word quietly while he lifted up the letters and pushed them back and forward in the palm of his hand. There was nothing but a quietly pronounced G and O and D.

He put the words 'Star of the Sea' together again, and thought of a star over the sea near Hamburg.

Uncle Bruno had driven to the sea.

Detlev remembers that he also repeated the words star of the sea to himself again and again.

Finally he said:

— Sea

and:

— Star.

The two words clattered like the typewriter in the municipal finance department. He took the words away for the last time.

He had cut off too many letters. It was difficult to push them all into the compartments. Detlev bent the fastener of the letter case over the lid.

Detlev woke up. The moon was sticking to the church tower. A full moon. A waning moon. A waxing moon. It wasn't a new moon. The moon shone on the cobble stones.

The siren howled. The sound rose from behind the black bushes in the churchyard. The moon shook from the howling in the clouds. The church tower shook above the shiny roof of the nave. The howling of the siren flowed over the church square. It hopped onto the window sills and scratched at the dormitory window panes. Detlev felt the howling in the cold bars of the bedstead. It slithered down the hall, up the stairs, past the enclosure, through the dining room, up the wooden body of the Lord Jesus Christ, over the balcony – here down the wall again, across the church square once again, up the church tower and turned the cross on top, the cock.

The siren sucked fog out of the black bushes, sand out of the joints in the walls, plaster fell from the ceiling in thin, white flakes. The siren sucked the coldness out of the graves in the churchyard, the damp, cold air out of the cellars, drew the air out of the tombs, out of the teeth of the skulls, drew the air through the orphanage, between Detlev's skin and Detlev's nightshirt.

Once the siren had reached the shaking moon, it slid down the church tower, crept behind the bushes, slipped under the cobblestones, ran between the pieces of coke, the briquettes, the bones, the preserving jars. The siren gurgled in the cellar for a long time. It gurgled like the water sprite in the book of fairy tales – not like the water sprite. It was a good water sprite. The siren gurgled in the square pit, under the cold tiles, by the lavatory.

— Air raid warning.

— Don't shout, we know that ourselves. You don't need to come from Hamburg to tell us that. We've got our own air raid warning. We know all about it. The Anglo–Americans are coming now.

— Where is the cellar? Where is my mummy? Where is the woollen blanket, the valerian drops. We have to go down the cellar quickly. Are you all wearing your pouches around your necks? The anti-aircraft guns will start shooting at once. The shell splinters are just as dangerous. They'll start dropping Christmas-tree flares and mines by parachute in a moment.

— They never come here. You're the only person here with one of those pouches. And there certainly isn't a cellar here.

— If you don't have a cellar then we're in deadly danger, perhaps then we'll even have to die.

— I don't want to die.

— I don't want to die either.

— I know what to do. We often used to do it in Hamburg. You have to stay quite calm and sit down on the floor. And when the bombs or parachute mines come down, you have to pull the woollen blankets over your heads – to protect yourselves against flying debris.

— We have to pray. But they never come here.

— Sister Silissa, Alfred says there's no cellar here. In Hamburg we all have a cellar.

— We don't believe that. Sister Silissa, Detlev says we have to sit down on the floor and pull the woollen blankets over our heads.

— What a terrible fuss that would be!

— They never come here, do they, Sister Silissa?

— If you pray hard, they'll never come here. Get dressed, we're going to the church. Our parish church is stronger than ten million air raid shelters and concrete bunkers put together. Detlev, you'll see that our parish church wards off any bombs – if any really do fall, but they never come here. If we all just pray nicely.

— Quick, quick, get dressed. We can pray over there. We must have some discipline. When the siren sounds every citizen has to seek out a bomb-proof shelter. For us that means the tower of the parish church.

Sister Appia looked from one to the other. Her black habit fluttered round the bedsteads. She stuffed Alfred's shirt into the back of his trousers. She gave Odel his jacket. She looked for Erwin's shoes under his bed.

Sister Silissa prayed in the doorway. From time to time she sprinkled holy water across the dormitory.

— Get dressed, damn it, get dressed. This is an air raid, said Sister Appia.

The children were silent. They pulled their things from the bedposts. Sister Silissa locked the holy water into the little cupboard by the door again. She looked past Sister Appia, because Sister Appia had sworn. Sister Silissa unbuttoned little Xaver's braces, untwisted them and buttoned them onto his trousers again.

Sister Appia said:

— Nit picker.

— Sister Appia, you lose your head because once a year we have an air raid warning. In our Fatherland there are towns which have air raid warnings twice a day and the people there stay calm and devout.

— But Siegfried is still standing there completely naked. If he doesn't get dressed from a sense of shame, he'll get dressed soon enough when the first planes crash onto the town. He's big enough to get dressed by himself.

Siegfried had slept in the orphanage that night. Little Xaver kept on his nightshirt under his woollen trousers. Odel buttoned up his jacket over his nightshirt.

Siegfried stood naked among the half-dressed boys. He wasn't even wearing a linen cloth. Detlev looked at Siegfried's skin from top to bottom. He saw the hair in Siegfried's arm-pits and the hair in the middle where the impurity began. Sepp in Steingriff had no hair growing there. The impurity hung down longer on Siegfried than it had on

Sepp. Siegfried turned round. He bent down. At the back Detlev saw, in the cleft above the legs, a thick black dot.

— That is the hole. You can't see your own hole. You should not. It is impure.

Siegfried said:

— I'm not going over the church at all. If bombs really do fall, then those shaky walls won't be any more use to us. My father says they never drop bombs here anyway.

Sister Appia struck him on the head with her fist.

— Now you see what can drop on your head. Into your trousers. And over to the church you go with all the rest. You're a typical only child. Just like someone else here.

— I'm ready quicker than the rest anyway.

Mother Superior called from the stairs:

— The lights must be put out. Otherwise we'll be the first to be bombed. Lights out, I say, the enemy formations are overhead. We'll only show them the way with our light. We're dragging the citizens who are observing the regulations into misfortune along with us. Do you want to be responsible for Bavaria being levelled to the ground?

— I can't see anything anymore, Mummy, because everything's dark, cried little Xaver.

— Your dear mummy can't save us any more now. Your mummy is running into the wood now, that's where it's safest. They don't drop any bombs on the wood. The deer and the snails don't need to be bombed.

— If there are munitions factories in the woods, they're strategically important targets.

— Be quiet, do you know who's standing behind the wall? Perhaps Kriegel is about, standing behind the wall, ready to take you away.

— We'll all be done for without your dear mummy.

— Only the Holy Mother of God can help us, said Joachim-Devil.

Odel and Alfred said the Ave.

— I hope they haven't brought any dive bombers with them. Then we don't even need to bother getting dressed.

The enemy doesn't have any dive bombers.

— Damn, I can't find my boots, damn.

— Erwin, don't swear.

— Sister Appia swore too.

— Shut up. Don't swear, I tell you. If Sister Appia dies in tonight's raid and hasn't sorted things out with her heavenly bridegroom first, then tomorrow morning she'll be jumping about in hell's frying pan.

— Anna swore. Anna is pulling on her dress now with the other girls in the girls' dormitory, thought Detlev.

Emerging onto the church square:

The sounds changed. The sound of steps, of arm movements, of the wind, of the crosses knocking to and fro on the nuns' stomachs. The sounds flew up as far as the moon. Down from the moon, from the stars trickled the sound of a moving tricycle.

— Be quiet. Keep together. Pray. Don't talk. The enemy aircraft don't hear your prayers. God hears them. . .

Detlev saw the silently spoken words of the prayers rising upwards – like the howl of the sirens – along the church tower up to the aircraft, which flew through the prayers without paying them any attention. The prayers were cut into pieces by the propellers and the wings, but they came together again behind the aircraft and flew higher, as far as the moon and past the moon, and flew into the great ear of God the Father, on which the stars were fixed like his grandmother's earrings. Detlev looked up. He saw the black sky and the stars that quivered from side to side.

He saw the moon which rolled forward across the sky like a lemon ice from the ice tongs in the café. Detlev heard the thin sound of the tricycle, of the enemy aircraft high above. He didn't see a huge ear. The orphanage children stepped into the shadow of the parish church which the moon cast onto the square. Sister Silissa opened the church tower door. Sister Appia led the way. It smelled of his grandfather's summer house, of the bran which was mixed with warm potato peelings for the hens, of insect powder, of tulip bulbs. It smelled of the compost heap, where the earthenware pot from the garden lavatory was emptied, where peat, lemon peel, piss, feathers and chickens' feet were mixed up together.

When the chemist's wife lay among the flowers at the undertaker's, her face all yellow, it smelled of his grandfather's compost heap. The orphanage children had filed past the dead woman because she and her husband had conferred great benefits on the orphanage. His mother paid the orphanage fees at the chemist's.

His mother didn't like the chemist because he had said that while the war was on, mothers shouldn't clean their babies' bottoms with cotton wool.

When the neighbour's four-year-old son died in Steingriff, Detlev hadn't seen the corpse. When Detlev went to school in the morning he saw, through the railings of the cemetery gate, the black mourners and the white child's coffin, which looked no bigger to him than the box for his mother's high boots.

When the butcher's assistant had committed suicide, the undertaker's room was covered with black hangings.

— He has a big blister full of water and blood on each hand. His face is blue. His tongue is hanging out.

When the gauleiter was laid out he didn't smell of his grandfather's compost heap. He smelt of the bread in the orphanage.

Frieda took Detlev's hand.

Frieda is Alfred's sister. She has promised Detlev the prayer of conversion.

Sister Silissa pulled the door shut and hooked the chain over a nail. She lit a match. She held a candle against it at an angle. The wick burned. Sister Silissa blew out the match. Close to

it her dark hand took on red edges. Drops fell from the ceiling
onto their hair and noses, onto their hands. No one prayed
anymore. Sister Appia lit a black candle.

They stood on the rectangular ground floor of the church
tower.

— Stand against the walls. It's safer and you've got something to lean against. It's safer, Detlev, isn't it?

Detlev thought about whether it was safer. In Hamburg
one couldn't stand against the walls. The cellar wasn't high
enough. His grandfather had to stoop. There were garden
chairs and camp beds along the walls. The package with the
first aid kit and the valerian drops lay on the draining board
for the washing. When there were air raids Mrs Selge came
with her sister-in-law, her two children and Mr Selge and sat
beside his grandfather, his grandmother, his mother, Detlev.
Once they had gone to a tall bunker. But no one liked it.
Some bombed-out families lived in the tall bunker all the
time. The men grumbled from cubicle to cubicle. The children were pushed through the low passageways in prams.
The Red Cross ladled out pea soup. A man held out a plate
of pea soup for Detlev. He said:

— It it.

He laughed, because it was supposed to be a joke. Detlev's
mother pulled him away.

— It's bad German. It should be: eat, eat.

When the concrete bunker rocked back and forward because
a bomb had exploded nearby, because a bomb had exploded
on the roof of the bunker, everyone was silent. After the raid
it was a long time before all the people reached the open air
again.

— I think it's safer if we stand against the walls.

— Detlev has been through it all before.

— We have to sypathize with Detlev.

Sister Silissa pushed the pearls of the rosary along. White
breath rose from mouths. The stones of the tower began

to hum. The nuns prayed loudly. Some girls prayed with them. The exhalations of white breath quickened. The nuns and the orphanage children didn't pray loudly enough. The humming grew stronger. Detlev felt it with his hands, with his back against the stones. The praying grew quieter. The humming remained. The nuns moved their lips without uttering any sounds. They pushed the rosary pearls along. The children stopped praying. They looked into the flames of the candles which their breath blew about from every side. The humming stopped. The nuns put the rosaries into the folds of their habits.

— Now it's over.

— I thought from the start it wouldn't last long.

The first bang had not been loud. The flames of the candles were no more restless because of it. Only when the breathing came faster did the flames flicker back and forward. Detlev felt the twitching in the stones. He looked up into the unplastered vaulting of the church tower. With every bang the vaulting sank down a little further on Detlev. Anna jumped towards the candles in the middle of the room. She wanted to bite herself in the hand. Sister Appia and Mother Superior held Anna's arms back.

— I don't want to burn.

Saliva sprayed out of Anna's mouth. She rolled her eyes, so that only the white was left between the lids. Anna tried to tear out her pigtails. Her knees banged together. She quietened down. The nuns let her slide to the ground. Anna fell asleep.

The bangs outside became neither louder nor fainter. They were repeated at regular intervals.

— They're falling on Munich or Donauwörth. That is our deliverance. They won't bomb Scheyern now. They haven't got that many bombs with them.

— You don't know that. The only person here who can say that is Detlev. He knows all about it from Hamburg.

Frieda placed her hand on Detlev's head. Detlev closed his
eyes.

Detlev closes his eyes.

The Feldherrnhalle is in Munich.

When they went on holiday his mother changed trains with
him in Munich.

There's a church with two towers in Munich.

The two towers burn.

In Munich the nuns and the orphanage children burn. The
nuns have red dresses and red veils and black faces and black
hands. They pop up and down in the flames like the teddy
bear his grandfather burned in the potato fire.

There's a smell of singed hair. There's no smell of compost
heap nor of orphanage bread. There's the smell of his mother's singed hair in the bathroom. She came too close to the
flame on the gas stove. There's the smell of the teddy bear's
hair. His grandmother said:

— It's wool. That's the test. You only need to burn a single
thread, then you know.

The nuns with the red veils fall out of the windows, from
the balconies in Munich; like the teddy bear, the children
fall zigzag from one burning pea plant to the next.

The beams bend.

In Munich all the cellophane pictures bend.

— The fire produces a great storm.

The storm lifts the roofs from the houses like a hand.

The columns of the Feldherrnhalle fall over.

The triangular gable ends, the windows, the stairs, the balconies fell across the table.

The teddy bear shrivelled up.

The teddy bears, the nuns, the orphanage children lie in a
long row. A firewood cross lies on each one of them.

After the battle the captain and the orderly lay the fallen in
a long row, before he packs them into coffins to drive them
home.

All are naked. Thick curly hairs grow in the middle of the white bodies.

The bodies are not white. The hair is burnt like wool. A long row of dolls. Baby dolls. Building blocks are tipped over the dolls. Thousands of dolls, building blocks, teddy bears. The dolls all roll their eyes like Anna. Detlev sees only the whites of their eyes. The dolls have nothing impure between their legs. The dolls are black like the teddy bear or they're red and green and blue like the wooden figure in the dining room. The arms and legs hang from the bodies on thin rubber bands. His mother had mended Peter with a sewing needle and a rubber band. Arms and legs lie among the crosses and building blocks like charred building blocks. Detlev can no longer count the beams with black and green heads, the dolls without arm beams and leg beams whose heads have been unscrewed.

Detlev opens his eyes again.

Detlev opened his eyes again.

No one says:

— Detlev, why do you close your eyes for half an hour like a sick hen?

Detlev closes his eyes. Detlev opens his eyes. Frieda took her hand away from his head. Detlev sank down. The siren pulled him up again.

— We prayed and that's why not a single bomb has fallen on Scheyern.

— In Munich they were just too lazy to pray, weren't they?

— Yes.

— If there were no Feldherrnhalle, if there were no air raid warning, if there were not three devils with the coffin, if there were no trip to Aichach, if he didn't eat ice with his mother on Sunday, then Munich wouldn't exist at all, there would be no hazel nut bush, there wouldn't be any hazel nut bush at all, Anna wouldn't have had any convulsions, I wouldn't have seen Sister Appia burn up, I wouldn't have seen the

Christs lying side by side in a long row like baby dolls with
broken off arms.

It's not over yet. Mother doesn't appear yet. The orphan-
age children and the nuns don't move. Siegfried is missing.
The cleaning woman isn't working in the orphanage to-
day.
Siegfried played with the orphanage children when his
mother came to do the cleaning.
There was also the fair.
Detlev didn't want to miss high mass because of the fair.
Detlev was afraid the orphanage children would shout:
— Detlev is missing high mass because of the fair. That's
how devout he is. He's a Protestant.
Detlev's mother said to him:
— At ten o'clock I'll be waiting for you at the back entrance
of the town hall.
Sister Silissa said to Detlev:
— Keep your eye on me during mass. I'll give you a signal,
so that you don't get to the fair too late.
Detlev had got used to the parish church. He had got used to
its shadow during the night and to the roof that glittered like
lametta in the moonlight, to the tower, to the bright yellow
walls of the tower in the sunlight.
Detlev had got used to the ribs and to the grey colour of
the rhubarb stalk vaulting. He wasn't frightened by the
pale face of the tall priest any more, he wasn't frightened
any more if the hoarse priest – after he had been speaking hoarsely for a while – suddenly began to shout. Detlev
knew the words and the melodies of the hymns. He knew
when to cross himself, he crossed himself with the same
dexterity as the Catholics, he knew how often the teacher
went to holy communion. Detlev had seen the bishop reading mass.

— The bishop trips as he walks, said his mother.

All the benches were full during high mass. Farmers who had come to town for the fair sat on the orphanage children's benches. The orphanage children had to kneel down on the left, half behind the altar.

Detlev was afraid of the brown rear-side of the altar. On Fridays, when the orphanage boys walked round behind the altar, singing, with candles in their hands, Detlev looked away, to the other side, at the coloured windows, where the saints, the Virgin Mary, the Lord Jesus with string, earthworms on his face and on his hands were illuminated by the sun.

Detlev was afraid that bones in boxes were lying around behind the altar, and the heads of saints, that spiders would be spinning webs across the eyes of saints, the eyes hung there in spiders' webs like marbles in little gauze bags.

Alfred whispered to Detlev:

— I heard what you've arranged with Sister Silissa. Of course, Sister Silissa doesn't know what you swore to the three devils. She doesn't know what awaits you if you're a hypocrite. You don't need to take my advice. It's nothing to do with me. But if you're looking over at Sister Silissa all through mass, instead of praying – it's not good. It's all the same to me. But it's certainly not good.

Each time Detlev looked away from the brown back of the altar, Alfred whispered:

— Don't look at Sister Silissa. Better not. It's all the same to me. Don't look.

Detlev imagined that Sister Silissa would make a signal, that he wouldn't see it, that his mother would wait and think:

— Detlev doesn't want to go to the fair with me. He doesn't want to eat an ice with me.

She would go away without him.

— No, she's coming right now.

What if she forgets? If she leaves him standing here with the dropping dirtying his hands? If the train left long ago? If she's forgotten that he's waiting here, in his Sunday things for the journey? If she forgets it, just as Frieda had forgotten the prayer of conversion.

Alfred said:

— Sister Silissa has nodded to you – despite her devotions. I happened to look up while I was praying. So I caught Sister Silissa's signal. I don't want to be the one to stand between your mother and your vow. You must know what you're doing yourself.

Detlev stood up.

— Detlev, you're exposing yourself to very great danger.

Detlev bent his knees in front of the altar.

— Turn round, Detlev. Or go. It's all the same to me.

Detlev tapped himself on the forehead, on his left shoulder, on his right shoulder, at his navel.

Between the rings of the bell announcing consecration, his sandals pattered just as they did on the concrete slabs in the garden in front of the house in Hamburg.

— Just let the devils come. Just let the devils come. Just let the devils come. Just let the devils come. As long as I'm with mummy they won't do anything to me.

Detlev did not run faster, faster, faster, faster between the arms, into the soft, flapping coat.

— Then they'll tear me back before I've got there.

Detlev walked more slowly with each step. He didn't breathe more rapidly. His mother came several steps towards him.

— Just let the devils come.

Then everything was warm and blue and soft and spinning.

— She'll be there right away. Then it will always be warm and blue and soft in her coat.

When she had swung him round in a circle, when he stood in front of her again, he said:

— I want to go home with you to granny and grandad.

— Come on, my little boy, come on. Now let's go to the
fair. We could have been together much earlier today. But
you had to run off to mass first. Were you afraid that they
would laugh at you or that you won't go to heaven or is there
some other reason?

— Perhaps mummy would rather that I was dead. Alfred said
it.

Detlev didn't say anything. Detlev saw his mother in front of
him one, two, three, four, five, six, seven times. His mother
with her long, warm hair and her soft skin and the hard
amber necklace in front of the birthday candles, his mother
with the wet apron and the burning hair in the bathroom.
His mother with her hair like a queen's in the train during
the evacuation, his mother with her arm stretched out at an
angle, his mother in front of the orphanage door, his mother
at the fair.

He saw his mother with other women in a row – beside the
chemist's wife, before she died, beside the three hovering
women with redcurrants in their hands, beside Sister Silissa
and Sister Appia and Mother Cecilia, beside his grandmother, beside Siegfried's mother, the cleaning woman,
beside little Xaver's mother – she works in the town hall too
– beside holy Mrs Weindeln.

— That is mummy. What's special about that?

The chairoplanes had been set up where the red-draped
block for the gauleiter's open coffin had stood.

— Would you like to go on the chairoplane?

— No.

— Are you frightened?

— No. I'm not frightened.

— Then have a go on it. You can have two rides, if you want
to.

The chain was hooked up in front of Detlev. When it started,
Detlev was overcome by fear. Odel had said:

— On the chairoplane it's like being in a dive bomber, you mustn't be frightened.

Perforated strips of paper rose and fell in a zigzag pattern below the pipes of the carousel organ.

Scheyern revolved. Detlev flew up high, far away from Scheyern. He couldn't distinguish the houses on the market place any more. He saw the trees beyond the roofs like green mushrooms by the town wall. A boy was hanging in front of Detlev. He flew in front of Detlev without the distance growing larger or smaller. The boy twisted round in the air. A girl was hanging behind Detlev. She screamed. Her face was wet with tears. She kicked out her legs. Detlev couldn't see his mother any more. The music grew more distant. Inside, in Detlev's chest, a heavy hammer struck against his ribs.

The music came closer. Detlev sank down in front of the military hospital, in front of the town hall, in front of the orphanage. His mother came up the wooden steps. The owner of the carousel unhooked the chain. His mother took Detlev's hand.

— We used to eat candy floss at the fairground, it looked like a huge pile of unspun wool. There was chewing gum too.

— What was it like? What did it taste like?

— Sweet. It was like rubber. You could put it in your mouth and chew it until it was soft. You could pull it out in a long string. If you let go, it jumped back into your mouth. You could blow bubbles with it.

— I'd like to have chewing gum.

— Don't be silly. Chewing gum comes from America. Germany is at war with America. So Germany can hardly import chewing gum.

— You brought me white chocolate once.

— You haven't forgotten that? The things you remember! That was at the beginning of the war. There's only white chocolate when there are no cocoa beans from overseas.

White chocolate is a substitute because of the war.

— You said it was something very special. I like white chocolate much more than brown chocolate.

— Now there's no white chocolate any more.

At the confectionery stall his mother gave the assistant her
ration card. He cut out two rectangles and filled a paper bag
with yellow sweets for Detlev.

— There isn't a nice fair in Hamburg at all. It's only got the
dirty, foggy Dom fairground.

— I want to go to Hamburg with you to granny and grandad.

— Granny says: Children who won't obey don't get to play.
Come over to the swing boat with me.

The boat in the swing boat was like a hat made of newspaper.
It was suspended from iron poles. Two men sat Detlev
between them.

— I hope you're not frightened — we want to go right over
with the swing boat.

—Don't make him frightened, we can't go right over at all.

— What if the men do go right over after all? If our heads
hang upside down, we'll fall onto the market place.

Detlev flew up with the two men, high above the parish
church, above Our Lady's Church, above the orphanage,
above the military hospital. He shrieked with the two men
as it came down again. He ground his teeth and crouched on
the floor when the men swung the boat up again.

— Dive bomber pilots dive down on the town and bomb the
town hall and the parish church and Our Lady's Church and
the orphanage and mother and the nuns and the orphanage
children and the pale priest and the short priest and Kriegel
and Anna and Alfred and Joachim-Devil and Otto. How nice
it is, when everything is broken to pieces. Mummy would
rather I was dead. Down it goes. Up it goes. Everything is
broken to pieces. Nothing is left of Aichach and Scheyern
except bare rafters like on the picture with the Führer. And
I fly away high above it.

Across the market square below moved three black, flapping, rounded dwarves followed by brown, grey, yellow, green ones. The swing boat braked.

— Let's leave the fair quickly. They're coming from the orphanage with the nuns. I want to go away to Hamburg.

— You've got no cause to say only bad things about the orphanage.

— I never said anything bad.

— The sisters do what they can to make life pleasant for you. They put an egg in the soup. When you're ill, they do everything they can to look after you. They even give you brandy and red wine in egg cups to drink, so that you grow strong and healthy. They may be Catholic, but they are good. Don't worry about silly Alfred with his sheep's face. His brother Shaky is much friendlier. And you don't want to live without Frieda at all any more. And Rosi? And Siegfried? How would you feel if you couldn't play with any of them any more? – My dear brother Vexed has everything he wants, but what he wants, he hasn't got and what he's got he doesn't want, my dear brother Vexed has everything he wants. You're allowed to go to mass every morning. You see things that no Protestant boy has ever seen before. Mother Cecilia shows you things in the convent that not even a Catholic is allowed to see. You should complain.

Detlev took her arm and pulled her through the arcade, away from the market place and the fair. At his mother's there was oatmeal cake again.

— Next time, bring a piece for me with you.

Everything becomes even slower. Detlev sees individual parts of movements, hears fragments of words.

Back to back, like the clouds of which his grandfather said:

— These clouds are called fleecy sheep clouds.

sheep blocked the road. Detlev and his mother parted the flock with their hands, with their knees. The necks were bent back, the sheep were pulled by the ears, pushed with

their knees. Their hands shone with oil. The bodies of the
sheep lifted Detlev's and his mother's feet off the ground.
Detlev and his mother swam across to the veterinary surgeon's house.

Detlev picked up the oatmeal cake, which wouldn't be there
if the bird dropping wasn't there, if he hadn't come to this
orphanage. He held the thick, triangular, brown piece of cake
in his hand. He lifted it to his nose.

— Nice cake. Not everyone has cake. Alfred doesn't have
any cake. Granny bakes cakes for me. The sisters don't
bake any cakes – only pancakes, which are three times as
thick as granny's pancakes in Hamburg. The pancakes in the
orphanage taste like flattened horse droppings on the road to
Steingriff.

The oatmeal cake smelled of dried rabbit skins. The whole
street smelled of oatmeal. The air which blew through the
veterinary surgeon's house smelled of rabbit skins.

— The veterinary surgeon has a rock garden. Where there
are lizards. If you hold a lizard by its tail, it falls off. Snakes
change their skin once a year. Then a snake made only of skin
– quite light – lies in the garden. One can even tell where the
eyes were.

The stairs smelled of oatmeal too, and the door, the wood of
the door, the door handle, the doorframe, the beam on which
C and B and M was written in chalk.

It didn't smell of dried rabbit skins. It smelled of ersatz coffee
powder.

The piece of cake disintegrated into crumbly powder in his
mouth. His grandfather's letter was in a yellow envelope. His
mother took it out, changed her glasses; she read it out in a
loud voice.

— Hamburg–Stellingen, the sixteenth of October, nineteen
hundred and forty-two. Dear Lisbeth, as we've been having
very heavy raids again recently, I think it's as well for me to
send you an inventory of our moveable goods, so that you

have some idea what claims you can present to the assessment office if need be. It is, of course, impossible to include everything. Missing, above all else, is the house, and everything that's closely tied to the house, which can be estimated at around fifteen thousand Reichsmarks. Missing also, are the allotment and the stall and its contents, approximately fifteen hundred Reichsmarks. In addition there would also be the plot of land at about five thousand Reichsmarks. I have an identical inventory with my documents in the air raid shelter. Hildegart doesn't have one, since she is at greater risk than we are. Your things are included in the inventory. I've dispensed with a verification of the inventory, I think they'll believe us anyway. Let's hope and pray that we never have to use it. It will at least give you something to refer to, if it should ever be necessary. Affectionate greetings to you and Detlev from your father and grandad. Mother will add a few more lines. Look how nicely granny and grandad still write despite their age.

— What kind of writing is that?

— German or Gothic. At school you learn Latin script.

Detlev knew that the priest in church croaked in Latin.

— The Catholic priest sings in Latin, my Protestant granny writes in Gothic.

Detlev remembers every word. His grandmother wrote

— It rained a little during the night. Otherwise it was quiet. Alfred interrogated him. Detlev didn't remember anything more. He remembered, when his mother had sucked in air, when she had adjusted her glasses, when she had swallowed the saliva, when she had raised her voice, when she had lowered her voice.

— Repeat what was in the letter.

— Did your mother never read you out a letter from your grandad?

— Of course. More often than you think. What is that anyway – a grandad? No one says that here. Are you a Jew?

— My grandad is the father of my mother and my granny is
the mother of my mother.
— And the father of your father and the mother of your
father?
— That's not my grandad and it isn't my granny either.
— Because you don't have a father. Was your father a Jew?
— What is a Jew? You don't have a father yourself. You don't
even have a mother.
— What was in the letter?
The veterinary surgeon called his mother. She went down-
stairs. Detlev took the letter out of the yellow envelope.
His grandfather wrote in Latin.
— Grandad is Protestant and writes in Latin, in which the
parish priest sings and in which the sisters pray in their
enclosure.
Detlev read the first sheet once again. He read the second sheet.
— You won't be interested in that. It's only figures. They'll
go in one ear and out the other again. They're just something
for me to refer to.
Detlev remembered everything:
A Roman one, then five thousand six hundred, large R, large
M, below it four thousand one hundred and fifty, a stroke.
— That means: equals
Nine thousand seven hundred and fifty a curved line to the
side of all three numbers.
— Only grandad can draw such a nice curved line.
Along the edges of the documents in his grandfather's desk
behind the enamel windows there were many long, curved
lines, also headings twice underlined, three exclamation
marks one after the other, two snakes that had tied them-
selves together.
— What does that mean?
— It means law.
After the curved line was a five, then came something like
the two round glass eyes of the gas masks, which lay in

their shoe boxes for anyone, for any emergency. Between the round eyes of the gas mask was an oblique stroke.

A one, a gas mask, the word repayment, four, a comma, five, a gas mask, from, one, full stop, seven, full stop, forty-two, then: four, eight, seven, five, zero, three, nine, zero, zero, zero, stroke, four hundred and thirty-eight, dash, comma, dash,

— Chimney sweep, gas mask, coal man, stealing coal, ane hoose afore dwells the butcher, ane hoose efter dwells the tailor, ane hoose further dwells the murtherer.

Settlement, two full stops, Emil.

— When I'm in Hamburg, I'll visit my uncle Emil, if he hasn't been bombed out yet. Uncle Emil and Aunty Hilde live near the Catholic church in Hamburg, Grandad showed me the Catholic church. Uncle Emil worked for the customs too. Aunty Hilde has very elegant mahogany chairs.

— You're mad to buy mahogany chairs with the world the way it is at the moment.

Emil pays thirty-two Reichsmarks rent a month, period, inclusive of mortgage repayment I pay thirty-eight, comma, twenty-one Reichsmarks, full stop, in the end Emil has nothing, dash, I, or my heirs after thirty-eight years have an unencumbered plot of land, semi colon, perhaps you'll still live to see it, comma, Detlev certainly will I hope, period. I hope he'll be grateful, period, the charges are further considerably reduced by the produce from the garden, period, I would like Detlev to take up a profession, comma, that makes it possible for him, comma to look after house and garden.

— I want to be a priest.

And that you will be in a position, comma, to keep up the payments your father and grandfather, period.

— Did you read the letter after all? Did you understand it?

— Yes. What did the veterinary surgeon want?

— He's given me notice.

None of that would have happened, if Scheyern wasn't there, not the boxes of building blocks in the street in Munich or Donauwörth, the crumbs on his hand, the traces of bird dropping on his hand.
— Mummy, I want to go to Hamburg.
— Haven't you read what it says in the letter? I thought you wanted to be a Catholic priest?
— But I want to go to Hamburg with you.
— You can't become a priest in Hamburg.
— There's a Catholic church in Hamburg. Grandad showed it to me himself.
— Grandad won't allow you to change your faith.
— Frieda has promised me a prayer of conversion. Grandad has a lot less say than a father. Let's go to Hamburg. And the veterinary surgeon has given you notice.
— He put it: A woman with a son in the orphanage. An unmarried woman with a son. You do understand. We live in a religious town.
Alfred said:
— You know everything in the letter. You just don't want to know. Give me the oatmeal cake. Do you know what we did after you ran away from mass? We finished our prayers and then we went to the fair. Afterwards we were allowed to play at mass. Mother Superior brought the toy altar down from the loft. She unpacked all of the mass game and we were allowed to dress up like the priests at Christmas high mass. You could have been practising. But you'd already run out of the real mass.
— There would be no mass game. There would be no holy mass.

Siegfried isn't standing on the balcony.
Detlev closes his eyes: The buttons on Alfred's jacket disappear one after the other – no more Alfred at all. No more

Alfred's shoes.

Siegfried isn't standing on the balcony. Detlev closes his eyes. Siegfried stands behind his eyelids.

Siegfried isn't there because the cleaning woman doesn't come to clean today.

The cleaning woman was there. Siegfried stood by the church tower. Detlev stood at the orphanage door. Siegfried stood under the golden letters.

With closed eyes Detlev can see him clearly. He sees the whole of Siegfried's figure. He sees every detail, the eyes, the circles around the iris, the eye lashes, the nose, the nostrils, the forehead sloping back, the cleft in the chin.

When Detlev opens his eyes, Siegfried has disappeared.

When Alfred's shoes, the buttons on Alfred's jacket appear in front of Detlev, Siegfried fades away, and the golden letters he's standing beneath. Detlev still sees Siegfried as he's looking at Alfred's jacket, but when he counts the buttons, only the letters of Siegfried's name remain. Siegfried sat on the steps which zigzagged down to the church square from the girls' dormitory. A stairway made of building blocks: Three building blocks at the bottom, two blocks in the middle, one block at the top. Detlev sat down on the uppermost building block.

— Why have you come to sit beside me, Detlev?

— You're called Siegfried. Mummy read me the story. He was very brave. It's a beautiful name.

— I'm very brave anyway. Siegfried is the greatest hero of our nation. No one else here is called Siegfried anyway. And you want to become a saint or a parish priest?

— Who told you that?

— Everyone knows that.

Siegfried looked straight ahead. He pressed his lips together. He didn't say anything else.

Siegfried had a small stick. He struck the lowest step with it. Sometimes sand was thrown up. Then Siegfried had forced

the tip of the stick between the cobblestones – when he raised
the stick for the next blow, sand sprayed up.

Detlev remembers that he had talked for a long time.
Siegfried didn't look at him. Detlev didn't know if Siegfried
was listening to him.

But Detlev knows that he had talked very loudly.

Detlev remembers that during his conversation with
Siegfried the clouds parted, that it became very hot that
afternoon, that the sun radiated a very yellow light, Detlev
remembers the roughcast scratching his back, the smell of
the warm stones, Siegfried's clothes, he remembers exactly
the distances from the stairs to the orphanage entrance, to
Saint Joseph's Fountain, to the side door of the church, also
the buildings, the trees, hands, and legs all overlapping. It
all lies together in Detlev's head like a soup cube, small,
rectangular, compressed – or like a shiny Christmas bauble.
Siegfried's right side is reflected on its silvery surface, large
and distorted.

In this round compressed mass of stones, smells, movement
that Detlev is trying to draw apart – there are words, sentences, Detlev's words from that day:

— I wanted to be a saint. Alfred and the others said I have
to be humble. Otherwise I'll go to hell. That's what the three
devils said. Mummy says: Don't forget you're a Protestant.
Grandad wants me to take up a profession so that I can
look after the garden. Recently I missed playing at mass. I
should have practised. I won't even be allowed to ring the
little bells as altar boy. I told one other person about it, that
was Anna.

— Anna's epileptic.

— What's that?

— It's material that doesn't deserve to live anyway.

— Anna betrayed me, because she was afraid of going to hell.
I know you won't betray me, you're called Siegfried. After
Anna had betrayed me, Alfred and the other two played

at being the devil. They wanted to put me in the coffin. They spoke through combs and paper, and Odel shouted into his pisspot. I didn't believe them. But Mrs Weindeln has seen Jesus and Mary. Properly with hands and ears and with clothes and shoes. You don't know what it's like when the devil comes. He scratches along the wall. He bangs on the washroom door and hammers and hammers, and because you're frightened you promise everything he wants. They lifted the coffin lid up, to force it down on my head. The air raids on Munich are nothing but the devil's work too. I've seen it in Hamburg. During a raid the devil tears people's arms and legs off. Lord Jesus Christ hasn't appeared to me. Everyone knows what he looks like. At consecrations he's there every time and at holy communion you even get to eat him. I don't really know what's happening any more. The devils said that I had painted the Christ Child with something impure between his legs. It was only a leg. The Christ Child was swinging it through the air. The devils come to me. Alfred asks me if I'm a Jew. I want to go to Hamburg to granny and grandad.

Siegfried said:

— You're all at sixes and sevens. Sometimes you talk about a devil, sometimes you talk about three devils, and about Alfred and Odel as well. What is a pisspot anyway?

— Piss means pissing and pot means pot.

— Whoever speaks like that? Are you really not a Jew?

— In Hamburg everyone speaks like that. Anyway, I don't even know what a Jew is.

— Why are you in the orphanage then?

— Because my mother is always being given notice.

— Why is your mother always being given notice?

— Because my father's dead and people don't like mothers without fathers who are alive.

— That's true anyway. But why aren't you living in Hamburg?

— Because lots of bombs are being dropped there. I want to go to Hamburg

— Why don't you want to stay here? We could become friends anyway. Because you're my man.

— I'm not a man at all. If the devils come again and you're sleeping in the orphanage, you'll be frightened too.

— Odel and Alfred and Joachim–Devil howled into the chamber pot, they're telling everyone now. Only they don't tell you. And the bombers, they're the Anglo–Americans and not devils.

— I know that just as well as you.

— Why are you afraid of them then, as though they were real devils?

— Because they sound like real devils. Because they behave like real devils. You would be frightened too, even if your name is Siegfried.

— Not me. From now on I'll protect you anyway. Alfred only wants to make you dependent on him with his lies.

— And when the bombs fall and the people are trapped with the briquettes for days, and they have to be pulled out with broken off arms and legs, and the dead are laid out along the street in rows, as granny says, and lime is sprinkled over them. You're not frightened when you're in the middle of all that?

— Not me anyway. I walk through the cemetery at night. I stayed alone in the room with the corpse of my dead uncle. Apart from that, the bombers never come here anyway. To Munich and Hamburg – but there are no strategically important targets in Scheyern.

— Yes there are. In the forest. I saw a truck which drove slowly because it was loaded with munitions.

— I don't care if the devil himself is flying the enemy bombers.

— The air raids aren't the worst. You sit together with lots of other people, and when it gets more dangerous, you get valerian drops, and grandad looks out to see if anything has happened yet. But the worst thing is if you wake up in the middle of the night, and the moon's shining, and the others are fast, fast asleep, and you can hear the devil under your bed. He's got very big ears and he's got a very big wart on his nose. The wart grows bigger and bigger and bigger. It starts to twinkle and spins round on his nose.

And what if the devils crept into Alfred and Odel and Joachim-Devil while they were sleeping and made their arms and legs move from inside and their mouths, like they do with Punch and Judy and with the crocodile whose mouth you can snap open and shut?

— If I protect you, perhaps you can become a saint or at least an altar boy.

— I don't want to be protected by you.

— I'm stronger than you. I need a comrade-in-arms.

— You won't protect me without asking for something. You're not in the orphanage often enough.

— I want to come more often now. Alfred must be overthrown. That's all. You should overthrow Alfred. Me too. And you. The only other person who could try to seize control is Erwin, but Sister Silissa loves him. He's got his hands full trying to get hold of extra eggs. Alfred makes everyone dance to his tune. He's built himself a bunker made of wooden stakes in the wood. A couple of years ago he escaped with Shaky and Rosi and Frieda and lived with them in his wooden bunker for weeks. If they hadn't run out of food, they would still be sitting there and scaring the whole district. They want to kidnap their enemies and take them to the bunker and kill them or at least torture them.

— When we had to pick herbs for tea for the wounded with the school, Alfred wanted to mislead me. He filled my net full of green stuff and they weren't herbal teas at all. At school the teacher had to throw everything away again.

— You fall for every piece of nonsense. You see, that's

how bad Alfred is. You could have gone to prison for that. Just think, handing in fake herbal teas. What if our poor, wounded soldiers had died from them? We'll overthrow Alfred anyway. We'll have to seize the wooden stake bunker right away, then no one else can get the better of us. Then we'll be the ones in power and we'll make sure that we eat eggs every day. Now I'll tell you what your tasks are.

First go quietly, very quietly, to the girls and tell them that they're really helping Sheepface when they're helping his sisters. Perhaps the girls will start to cry and want to run to his sisters, then you'll have to calm them again and praise Alfred a little and say that they should just hold out a little longer, some things are going to change soon anyway. You can go to Frieda and Rosi and tell them how much their brother uses them and ask whether they don't want to support you and the new government, because you're the nuns' favourite anyway.

— Sister Appia doesn't like me.

— She just can't show it. After that you go to the weak ones and to the little ones and stir them up against Alfred. Things are going to be different soon. So you run back and forth and puff up one lot with the others. If Alfred gets wind of it, just tell me. I'll be back when I'm needed. You have to try and make his brother abandon him. Shaky can't stand up straight. But he's a good spy. When they're all against Alfred, we'll have the upper hand, and I'll fight with him just once, to show him that by himself he's nothing at all. I'll win and we'll be in charge. Now I have to go home.

The cleaning woman came towards Siegfried from the orphanage door.

— I have to go with my mother now, back home to my father. Where is your father?

— My father is dead.

— My father is big. He's very strong.

— My father is bigger than your father.

— Isn't yours dead? My father can thrash everybody.

— Does a father often hit his children?

— That depends. Mine doesn't. He doesn't hit my mother either.

— But my father is big and much stronger than the church tower. My father is so big, that he touches the clouds.

— That's impossible. Detlev is talking nonsense.

Siegfried's mother gave Siegfried a shove. That was supposed to mean:

— Come on.

— Don't forget what you have to do.

Siegfried's mother went away with Siegfried.

Siegfried beside his mother. Siegfried in front of his mother. Siegfried by Saint Joseph's Fountain. Siegfried under the golden letters. Siegfried reflected in the shop for devotional articles. Siegfried full of rosaries.

Siegfried didn't come back to the orphanage until one or two weeks later. In the half year he slept three, four times in the orphanage.

Two pairs of wrestlers:

The group in front of Detlev parted.

The fighters came forward.

Alfred, Siegfried.

Detlev, Xaver.

Siegfried isn't there. The group in front of Detlev gets mixed up. Legs with striped socks appear next to faces. Arms grow beside other arms, arms grow between thighs, legs grow beside ears.

A ball of legs, heads, arms, hands.

The dragon on the cover of the book of legends has eight green legs.

Detlev saw the legs from the floor, Xaver's boots above his nose. Alfred's head hung between Siegfried's knees.

Siegfried's face stuck to Alfred's hips. Siegfried's head between Alfred's knees. Alfred's face on top. Four legs. Four
arms. God didn't help Siegfried.

Siegfried is wearing pink trousers and has a yellow shield in
his hand.

— It's yellow shield, not yelly shield.

There was nothing of the Lord God or the Virgin Mary
to be seen on the cover. The green dragon writhed under Siegfried's feet. Siegfried writhed under Alfred's knees.
Detlev writhed under the sole of Xaver's right shoe.

When Detlev had told Frieda about her brother's wickedness, she said:

— You're devout. I know how bad Alfred is. Why do you
want to revenge yourself on him? You don't need to. You're
devout. After our mother had died as well, Rosi, Shaky and
I agreed to regard Alfred as our father and mother.

Detlev went to Rosi. She said:

— None of us dares to do anything against Alfred any more.
No one wants to argue with him. Rosi gave Detlev a picture
of a saint. Detlev began to forget what Siegfried had told
him to do.

— I want to get my revenge on Alfred.

Detlev tried to get Anna by herself. She ran away from him.
When he approached, she quickly joined the other girls and
turned her back on him.

Detlev met her on the stairs alone. He spoke to her. She
turned her head to the side and looked up and blinked.
Detlev said something about the new times that would
begin in the orphanage because of Siegfried. Anna didn't
stop blinking. Before Detlev could finish talking, other girls
came, and Anna ran off with them. Detlev followed the girls.
They hid in the girls' dormitory.

— Boys aren't allowed in the girls' dormitory.

Detlev didn't know how he could unobtrusively begin a
conversation with the other girls about Alfred's wickedness.

Alfred often followed Detlev when he went over to the girls'
table. Detlev quickly took Jochen and Aloys aside in the
washroom.

— It's about Alfred.

— Is there something to complain about again?

— Alfred is very bad. Things have to change.

— He's got a sheep's face.

— If he does something to you, tell us, we'll help you.

Jochen ran off to his master in the smithy. Sister Silissa came
to hear Aloys sing 'In March the farmer yokes the horses'
before going to school. When Detlev accompanied Odel to
school, he considered whether he should tell him, someone
who had played the devil, about the plans. He asked why
Odel had played the devil.

— I didn't want to have a fight with Alfred. That's why I
helped him. Then I had to laugh when you screamed for
your mama.

— Alfred does what he likes with us. He's evil.

— Yes, he's very evil. But he's the best. Everything's fine the
way it is.

Detlev didn't dare talk to Shaky. Alfred made fun of his
brother's waddling walk. When Alfred was gone, Shaky
cursed Alfred. Shaky questioned the little boys on Alfred's
behalf, where they hid their cellophane pictures, their
sweets, their chalk pencils, and after Shaky had reported
back Alfred stole them. Alfred had promised his brother a
reward for spying, but afterwards Shaky begged for it every
time in vain. The victims didn't go to Sister Silissa to inform
on Shaky and Alfred. And Shaky who had been cheated
didn't go to any of the nuns either to inform on Alfred.
Shaky started to spy again, as soon as Alfred promised him
some of the spoils.

Joachim-Devil said to Detlev:

— I can smell it, there's going to be a rebellion.

— Are you planning a rebellion, Joachim?

— Not me. But there's something like it in the air.
— Alfred protects us all. No one's planning a rebellion. Perhaps you are? Has Alfred hurt you?
— I don't want a rebellion. I thought you were planning a rebellion with Siegfried. You would have very good reason to take your revenge on Alfred. I haven't got any reason. I'm too weak.
— I'm also too weak. Siegfried and I alone are also too weak.
— Three weaklings don't make one strong man.
Joachim-Devil ran away.
Detlev explained everything to little Xaver at length. Like Detlev, little Xaver had a mother who worked in the municipal finance office and only came to visit the orphanage at weekends.
Little Xaver said:
— I don't know nothing. I'm not joining anything.
The next time, the cleaning woman was without Siegfried. The time after that Siegfried came with the cleaning woman.
— Have you prepared everything?
— It was difficult. I tried hard. It's such a long time since you were here. Now you have to do something. I think you can take power now.
Siegfried looked for Alfred. He walked up to Alfred.
— You, it's going to be settled today.
Alfred tried to talk Siegfried into a bout of finger tug. Detlev was afraid that Siegfried would agree. No one in the orphanage was as good at finger tug as Alfred.
— Finger tug is for girls. A free fight.
Before the fight, Alfred and Siegfried took the knives and the catapults and the handkerchiefs out of their pockets. Alfred wanted to hand everything over to Detlev, for him to put them down on the table. Detlev accepted Siegfried's things and laid them to the side. Alfred had to wait until Shaky took something from him.

— I'll pay you back for that. For not taking them, said Alfred to Detlev.

The circle closed around the fighters. The onlookers climbed up on the benches, up on the table, up on the window sills. Detlev leant against the big crockery cupboard. Below in the compartment by the pots, sat the new boy. He pulled the sliding doors shut from the inside and banged his doll against the slats.

Detlev heard him shouting:

— Youking. Youking.

Detlev thinks:

— Peter has disappeared forever.

The fight began. Detlev prayed.

— Only Catholics like us can pray.

— How do you pray?

— Properly.

— What's properly?

— We talk to God and he hears us.

— Do you talk in a special way?

— No, only inside, without saying it out loud. And we don't think about anything else while we're doing it.

— I can do that too.

— But God doesn't hear you.

Detlev prays:

— Dear Father which art in heaven, make Siegfried win, that is our salvation. Amen.

— Blessed Mother of God in heaven, don't let Sister Silissa or anyone else come in now. Our brother is about to win, cried Frieda.

— Watch his knee. Just push it down Alfred.

— Mary and Joseph, the sweatbox is doing Siegfried in, shouted Shaky.

Rosi cried:

— Damn it, our Holy Father in heaven wanted it this way: Our brother is winning.

Detlev couldn't think of any more words for his prayer. While he repeated the words, he thought of Frieda, Shaky, Rosi, of Siegfried and Alfred. He didn't think anything particular about them. He saw their figures in front of him, he saw them raise their hands and their mouths opening and shutting.

Detlev heard Siegfried's voice from the sweatbox saying:

— Alfred, if you let me go and if you don't ride back and forward on my arms and legs and if you don't give me any Chinese burns, I'll tell you everything, and I'll give you my knife.

Siegfried fell from Alfred's arms.

Everyone turned round – not to Detlev – in the pause, in the silence Peter came crawling out of the crockery cupboard and struck his doll on his table.

Detlev fell on his back.

— Xaver, hit him on the nose.

— Little Xaver is hitting big stupid silly Detlev on the nose with his hard fist.

— Detlev is falling down.

— There's spunk in Xaver's little legs.

— Bite his ear, Xaver.

Someone struck Detlev's knee.

— God's judgement.

Detlev looks down at his legs. They're thinner than Odel's legs – no one can see the nuns' legs. Detlev's legs are fatter than Xaver's legs, standing upright on his stomach.

— There's no use in praying any more. Hit him on the nose till it bleeds. It's too late for that now as well.

— The Lord God is punishing Detlev.

— Detlev is seven. Little Xaver is five.

— Detlev's already eight now.

— The Lord God has chosen little Xaver to beat Detlev.

Alfred had set the smallest boy on Detlev. Alfred and Shaky and Rosi had praised little Xaver's every blow. Frieda had been silent. She hadn't warned Detlev about a single blow, she hadn't told him of a single clinch.

— Detlev was always just a Protestant.

— He only came here from Hamburg, to eat up our bread.

— Your bread smells of dead gauleiter.

— Oh, just listen to him.

— He'll be taken to the devil's bunker now as punishment.

— That's the death bunker.

Alfred knew everything that Siegfried and Detlev had agreed. Siegfried had confessed everything.

— Why did he tell it all? He could hardly stop himself. He even made up things as well.

The shoe grows larger and larger until it covers the tangle of arms and legs and heads behind Detlev's eyelids – one small black patent leather shoe on the end of the striped sock on Xaver's right foot.

Xaver kicked Detlev in the face.

Detlev didn't move. It hurt less than he had expected.

— The prisoner is being kicked in the face.

— The criminal kicked the postman with the registered letter in the face.

— Mummy has Nivea cream.

— Three days rain. Three days sunshine.

— Detlev isn't moving any more. He's been so beaten for his sins. He doesn't wipe the sand from his face.

— Detlev won't want to tell Sister Silissa anything about his defeat.

— Detlev will be humble now at last.

— Detlev is going to accept everything now.

— I didn't scream. I didn't cry. My nose didn't run. I didn't flail about.

He became stiff, pushed onto the bottom shelf of the crockery cupboard, like one of his grandmother's plum tarts. They closed the doors from the outside.

He stood alone in front of the house in which the cockerel foot soup was cooking. It was evening. Children with lanterns came. His mother didn't come. She had been wearing the amber necklace when she left.

Chairs, shoes, tin plates, books, building blocks were thrown against the doors. Beacon flames leapt up with each explosion. Detlev warmed the air between the wooden walls.

— That's what it's like when you die in a cellar. I'm not frightened. I want to go to Hamburg. Because the Anglo-American bombers will soon come to Scheyern and then nothing will be left.

Sister Silissa opened the doors. Detlev was supposed to crawl out.

— He likes going in there.

— It was my own idea to go in there. It's fun.

When they wanted to push him in the next time, Peter crawled in instead of Detlev.

Inside Peter shouted:

— Youking. Youking.

In the evening, before going to sleep, he ran around in the dining room with his doll, struck the doll's head on the table, against the walls.

Then the others said:

— Now you have to go in again.

He went, without them needing to push him, onto the bottom shelf beside the pots. He closed the doors himself from the inside.

During the time that Peter spent in the orphanage, they forgot Detlev. Peter was taken away. Alfred questioned Detlev:

— What did your mother do to you? What did you tell her?

— She didn't do anything to me. But I told her: I want to leave. I want to leave. I want to leave. Detlev shouted the four words more and more loudly. First he shouted them down at the floor, then they struck Alfred's face, finally they shot right across the dining room to the girls at the opposite window.

Now all that remains of the words is a few movements of the lips. The words fill up his whole head. They make the muscles around his head move. They make his jaw move. A few letters are formed by his lips. They aren't even spoken out loud.

Detlev thinks:

— Now Alfred is thinking: Detlev is remembering that he shouted: I want to leave. I want to leave. I want to leave.

— Now Alfred is afraid of me.

Frieda called:

— Are you tormenting Detlev again. You tormented Peter so much that he had to be taken away to an asylum.

Detlev thinks about Marie in Steingriff. She always wore the same blue dress. It was never dirty. It was never freshly ironed. Perhaps Marie's mother washed it in the evening and hung it over the stove at night to dry or Marie never dirtied her dress.

Marie had black straggly hair. No one in Steingriff hit her, no one laughed at her, no one ran behind her. She walked very slowly and at every door she had to think for a long time whether she should go in. She spoke little and slowly and quietly. She lived with her mother in the last house in the village on the main road. Together with her mother she did outwork. They packed little tubes full of ointment into boxes. The boxes were sent to the front. The ointment hardened on wounds. It disinfected the wounds and sealed them from dust and rain. Detlev opened a tube. The ointment smelled like all-purpose adhesive. Everything turned black in front of Detlev, then he saw white plum trees. The ointment was fluid and clear. The boys in the village stuck the paper parts of their model planes with all-purpose glue. Detlev wished he could have cut-out sheets and adhesive and thin wood, so that he could build a Stuka or a Fieseler-Storch. He would have known exactly what an aeroplane looks like inside. Detlev saw himself flying up in a Stuka, flying down, engines off, bombs away, bombs away.

— I don't want anything like that in the house. If they find that in our house, they'll end up saying we've been spies.

Once a fortnight a lorry came to Marie's mother and took away the packed tubes. Boxes of unlabelled and unpacked tubes were unloaded.

Marie was taken away in the lorry. Marie died in the asylum. Her mother had to travel there and collect a black urn full of ashes. The boys in the village had different versions. The urn was sent to Marie's mother's house by post.

The friend of Detlev's mother had been burned, before the war. At the cemetery. She had chosen that herself before her death. The friend's mother placed the urn with the ashes in her display cabinet. A bomb fell on the house.

— My friend's ashes had mingled with the ashes of the house.

Frieda said to Alfred:

— You know what's happening to Peter now. Why do you torment everyone? It was you who made Peter really crazy. He ran around with his doll, shouting: Youking. – That didn't hurt anyone. It didn't even bother anyone.

— No one had any idea what it was supposed to mean.

— It was supposed to mean: You King. Anyone could work that out.

— What kind of king?

— The King of the Jews, of course. Our Lord Jesus Christ.

— You shouldn't say it like that, Frieda. It should be, the King of Christendom.

— Peter eavesdropped at the door of the enclosure, when the nuns were reading the Christmas plays to one another. They're already preparing everything now. That's where Peter picked up the word king.

— Eavesdropping at the enclosure isn't allowed.

Frieda pulled Detlev over to the girls' table. She lifted him onto the bench and sat down in front of him. She was sewing.

Between the stitches she talked to Detlev. There was a long pause if she had to cut the thread and look for the scissors. She stretched the word out when she drew the thread up into the air after a stich.

— You want to backslide, Detlev. Do you really want to travel back to Hamburg, to the land of the Protestants? They don't have the proper faith. Incense is too dear for the Protestants. The priests don't wear beautiful clothes. There are no altar boys and little bells. You want to run away from the tests that God is setting you. You're disheartened, but you were chosen to become a priest and perhaps even a bishop with a gilded, pointed hat. Now you're going back and don't want to continue on the difficult path. You could have raised yourself above your sins and would have entered Paradise. I know that for certain. Why are you so short of breath? The cross is heavy for every one of us. Yours is so heavy for you because you are only eight and because you don't know anything about your father. But the Virgin Mary and the Lord Jesus Christ have chosen you for something higher. We are already hard-pressed enough, and we'll never amount to much. We have no father and no mother any more. My brother Alfred is corrupted and torments everyone wickedly, Shaky walks like a duck. He'll never amount to anything, because even before he's started something, everyone's already laughing at him. Alfred will end up a burglar. That's what I think, and Rosi is as thick as a plank. We are not alone with our misfortune. You are not alone with your misfortune. Anna has fits, and who knows how long she'll be allowed to have her fits in peace. Even the holy sisters have to struggle and die like everyone else in the end. They don't ascend to heaven with bones and flesh. They have to let their hair be cut off. They aren't allowed to have a single hair under their coifs. Every Sunday they have to soap their bald heads and shave each other's stubble off. Sometimes they cut each other and one can see the spots of blood on the white coifs.

The archbishop trips as he walks, as your mother puts it, and the Pope gets hiccups. Even Kriegel has his cross. If Kriegel doesn't squeeze the work out of the Poles, then the people from the Party will dismiss him and whip him and his wife and children worse than he whipped the prisoners of war. The priests bear the heaviest cross at this time. But some throw it off, as you want to throw it off, and preach shooting to kill at mass, and lick the arses of the people in the Party. But they'll lose eternal bliss for that, for in the Bible it says: Thou shalt not kill. And when Peter had cut off the ear to defend Lord Jesus Christ, Jesus lifted it up and stuck it on again. Don't complain, Detlev, think what the orphanage has saved you from. Think how terrible the air raids in the distance sound. Just think how many little boys have died under the ruins! Think about Peter, whom they simply took away – and no one knows what will happen to him and how many are being taken away like Peter. No one has taken you away, because the sisters love you very much. And if all that can't dissuade you, if you still believe you're suffering too much, then think of your mother. You don't need to explain anything to me. She stayed behind here after the evacuation because you're safer in Scheyern. That's why she moves from one apartment to another, because there are difficulties if she stays in one place too long. No doubt it's all because of your father, Detlev.

— My father's dead. My father's name ended in Schitzki or something.

— The Schritzkis and the Schinskis and the Schitzkis all change their names when they join the Party. Then instead of Schitzki their names end in Burg or Dorf or Hausen.

— My father's dead. My father wouldn't have changed his name because he was frightened. My father was strong and as big as a giant. Bigger that your father.

— Finally, your mother has hidden herself away in a tiny room. She wasn't allowed to keep you there with her. Then she was given notice anyway. She put you in the orphanage so that you're safe if anything should happen to her.

— If anything should happen to her? If she falls and cuts her knee? If she breaks her leg? Someone pushes her to the ground? Then we'll miss the train. If she's been arrested? If she's died? Mummy doesn't miss any trains. Mummy doesn't die. Nothing will happen to mummy. She's walking across the market square right now.

— She would never have parted from her boy voluntarily. But you want to be weak and give up your priestly calling – only because Anna betrayed you once, because the three of them played the devil, because Siegfried is a dishonourable coward and because you didn't want to defend yourself, when they set little Xaver on you and they told him every hold. That isn't sufficient reason to give up God. As a priest you would look like an angel in mourning.

— Why doesn't God come, when the bricks fall on the babies and their bones are turned to pulp? Why doesn't he hold out his hand to stop them? Why doesn't he put a hole in the tyre, when the lorries come to take away Marie and Peter?

— I don't know. No one can know that. Be grateful that you've been saved until now. If you really must go to Hamburg – I'll give you a prayer of conversion to take with you. You only need to say it once a day – preferably before you go to sleep – then you'll gradually become a Catholic and in the end you'll be able to take holy communion and become a priest, perhaps even an archbishop – a holy person in any case.

But look into yourself, Detlev. Don't grieve us, not Sister Silissa, Mother Cecilia, not me, not Joachim-Devil, who always looks up to you, and above all not your mother. Bear the cross. Don't go away. But if you do go, you'll get the prayer of conversion from me.

Frieda would not have bitten off the thread. She wouldn't have stood up and become very tall in front of him, wouldn't have looked down on him, not laid her hands on his shoulders. Detlev would not have said:

— Why doesn't God come and pull the babies out from under the rafters before their heads become pulp?

Frieda would not have promised him the prayer of conversion. Peter would not have been taken away – Peter and his bald doll. At first they wanted to take the doll away from him. But he screamed out loud. They let him keep the doll, so they could load him up with less fuss.

Peter would not have called his doll 'Youking'.

Frieda didn't say anything else. She had passed a new thread through the needle and was sewing without looking at Detlev any more.

— But the Christ Child does exist.

You only need to put a five pfennig piece in the slot above the fish tank.

It wasn't a fish tank, but it looked like a fish tank. The stars began to twinkle. Heaven's door opened. Little bells tinkled. The Christ Child came jerkily out of heaven's door. On the floor of the tank Detlev could see the groove with the pivot on which the Christ Child was mounted. He jerked forward in an arc along the groove to the glass wall. When he had arrived on the right hand side of heaven, the pivot swung the Christ Child round and he jerked back, through heaven's door again. Heaven's door snapped shut behind him. As the Christ Child jerked through the fish tank he moved his right arm. The Christ Child was made of tin. The right arm had a joint. The joint creaked as the arm moved. Detlev couldn't work out how the Christ Child operated the joint. The Christ Child raised his lower arm, his hand, lowered his hand to his stomach, brought his lower arm and hand to the left, drew his hand to the right. That was the blessing. He made the sign of the cross once when coming out of heaven's door, the second time in the middle of the heavenly firmament, the third time shortly before turning round at the end of heaven and three times on the way back. The Christ Child appeared each time Detlev dropped in a five pfennig piece. Each time he gave his six blessings. With his head against the fish tank wall Detlev wondered whether the gauleiter, before he died, had also put in lots of five pfennig coins, whether Kriegel, when he came from whipping Poles, was also blessed by the tin Christ Child. The Christ Child had definitely blessed Alfred, the veterinary surgeon, the chemist, the pale priest, the teacher and his mother when she had gone into Our Lady's Church with Detlev – on the day of their arrival, before they had seen Saint Joseph's Fountain.

The little bells tinkled, when the big bells in the two towers of Our Lady's Church rang. The little bells tinkled, as the bells from the towers were being broken. The Christ Child gave his blessing six times after each recorder lesson. He gave his blessing six times after the devil had come and after the Anglo-Americans had bombed Munich or Donauwörth.
— But the Christ Child does exist.

There was also the doll, which Peter called 'Youking'. There was the doll which Mother Augusta rocked back and forward as a substitute for the Christ Child, when she rehearsed with the wounded in the military hospital. The more beautiful doll was used during the performance. There was the beam of light over Herod's bed. The beam of light was the Christ Child. Herod was afraid of the beam of light. He had given the command to kill all the little children. That's why the Virgin Mary fled to Egypt with Joseph and Jesus.

Detlev no longer remembers exactly what happens in the play.

There was the Easter lamb which the sacristan's boy found in the bushes. They all looked down on the apse from the balcony. The lamb had a red ribbon round its neck. The sacristan's boy held the sugar lamb in his arms. He received the best Easter present, the Christ Child as Easter lamb, because he was the sacristan's son.

Detlev doesn't think every word through to the end. The pictures lie on top of one another like cellophane pictures. The lines cross over one another with different degrees of boldness.

The first letter or the first syllable of the words is enough, often a part of the first letter. Of the faces that are not present on the balcony, the nose is enough, the eyelashes, the hair. A noise is enough, a smell, a drop of rain.

The little ladder at the beginning of a song means:

— You must not forget to play an F sharp instead of an F.

Everything jerks past more quickly: The repetitions, the twice remembered speeches, the hardly varying actions, his mother's new room, his mother's face in the new room.

Detlev couldn't tell whether she was happy. She lived by a field at the edge of town. The road in front of the house was muddy.

It doesn't take much time to think about the new room – the smallest fraction of a part of the seconds between raising his little eye and his mother entering.

Detlev doesn't conclude that:

— To think about the hazel nut the second time, took as long as for the sun to fly from the edge of the cloud to the middle of the cloud – or: To remember the walk to Aichach, I needed just as much time as Alfred needed to look up from the floor to Sister Appia.

Detlev feels this whole year in his head like a dry soup cube, like a twinkling Christmas bauble, like the hazel nut, whose stalk poked out of the earth after it had been planted and which Alfred dug up and ate – this whole year in three, four, five, six seconds

— twenty-one, twenty-two,

in the moments between the squashing of the bird dropping and his mother entering.

The other recorder lesson. The same smell. There was no case for the notes as there was for the letters of the alphabet at school.

Detlev could read the individual notes of the songs like the individual letters of the story about the Führer's youth.

There was the Latin script of his Protestant grandfather. There was the Gothic script of his Protestant grandmother. There was the Latin speech of the Catholic parish priest. There was the Bavarian speech of the Protestant pastor in the small church outside the town wall. There was the Danish accent of Pastor Roagers in Hamburg. There was musical notation.

Detlev played the song 'Star of the sea I greet thee'.

Mother Cecilia said:

— It's in F-major.

After the treble clef a lime tree leaf hung among the staves.

— A lime tree leaf fell on Siegfried's back.

—It means that B-flat must be changed to B.

Detlev liked to finger the B:

The thumb of the left hand under the recorder – as support. Index finger, third finger on the first and third stop of the recorder. The middle finger up in the air. The right hand: only the index finger on the fourth stop.

The deep C sounded wrong. The lip of Detlev's recorder was worn.

— Mother Cecilia's recorder sounds gentle.

In his grandfather's garden Detlev had bent over a barrel which had dried out during the hot summer. Detlev had called into the barrel and the sound was like the sound of Mother Cecilia's recorder.

— The lip is the most important part of a recorder. But it's wartime. The wood that had been stored has been burned or it's being used for essential war production. There are no new recorders to be bought. Be glad that you've got a plastic recorder. Even if the lip is worn. Blow carefully. Cover nicely with your finger.

He played 'Deutschland, Deutschland, über alles, über alles

in der Welt'.

— I can't bear to hear it any more. But you must be able to play it. – Forget what I said.

It was in G-major. The F-sharp sounded wrong on the plastic recorder too. Mother Cecilia had got used to it, but Detlev started each time he had to play the F-sharp in 'Deutschland, Deutschland, über alles', or in 'Rose tree, sweet, bloom when I see my maiden'. He was not allowed to play 'The brittle bones tremble'. Mother Cecilia quickly turned over the pages in the recorder book.

They walked towards the hall door under the cross-vaulting. There were empty chairs in the hall. A nun sat in the middle of the room. She was reading a small notebook. At the raised end of the hall stood two nuns and three of the lightly wounded. The three wounded men were wearing field grey coats and pyjama trousers. Detlev should go up, ordered the nun with the notebook. She was wearing glasses and took them off when she looked at Detlev. One of the nuns on the platform rocked a baby back and forward. She sang quietly. She looked at the doll as if it was a living baby.

— Sing more loudly, called the nun with the notebook and the glasses from below.

The nun with the baby – with the doll baby – coughed and sang the song once more just as quietly.

— It's fine like that. – So you're called Detlev?

— Yes.

— Do you have some music with you?

— Yes.

— What can you play?

—'Listen, people, and hear the tidings', 'Silent night, holy night', 'Deutschland, Deutschland, übes alles', 'In March the farmer'. I could even play 'The brittle bones tremble'.

— You're a bright boy, but down here I can hardly understand what you're saying. Can you play, 'O little children come'?

— He'll have a go at it.

Mother Cecilia had climbed up and pulled out the music for Detlev.

— You must come down now, Mother Cecilia. You're spoiling the whole effect. Someone in the cast hold the music book. Franz, kneel down in front of Mary. Detlev, sit down further to the left. Franz, hold the music book.

The wounded soldier, who looked down when the nun with the glasses shouted Franz, had an arm that looked like a seagull's wing. Around his neck was a tyre made of plaster.

— Detlev, sit down on the bench.

Detlev sat down on the bench

— Begin playing.

Detlev made a lot of mistakes. The page trembled in the wounded soldier's hands. Detlev saw the thick brown hairs on Franz's hand beside the notes.

Detlev saw the pillars and bridges over the river Elbe. Seagulls flying under them.

— He still has to practise it.

— He mustn't make mistakes during the performance.

— No.

— While the shepherd plays the flute, Mary rocks her child. Gently back and forward. Quite naturally. Saint Joseph gives a kind smile. And the woman carrying water passes by at the back.

A nun walked past at the back.

— From the wings at the right – Go on. Go on. – come the three wise kings.

Three lightly wounded soldiers came through a door.

One had a bandaged finger. The second wore one thin and one clumpy shoe. Two of the kings took the third by the hand, pushed him till he knelt down and made the shapes of the letters with their fingers in front of his eyes.

The third king had bandaged ears.

Detlev imagined the nuns in the hospital painting the all-purpose glue, which crazy Marie and her mother had packed into boxes, on the wounds – on the soles of feet, on ears, on elbows – before Marie herself was driven away in the lorry, before she died, before her mother put the black urn in the display cabinet – beside the black edged identity card photo of her father who had bled to death in a military hospital.

In winter, people went sledging on Calvary Hill. When the nuns and the orphanage children walked between the snow walls which the snow plough had thrown to the side of the street, the veils and the habits looked blacker than in the orphanage, in the church, in the convent. People went sledging on the path that led past the stations of the cross. The nuns and the orphanage children walked past the back of the plaques on which the via dolorosa of the Lord Jesus Christ was pictured in coloured enamel.

When no snow was lying, one could see from the path the Last Supper, the Judas Kiss, Pontius Pilate, Golgotha. Bright. Pink, violet, orange, green, blue, yellow.

— The colours are greasy. The colours are mixed with snot.

— You mustn't blaspheme. It's enamel.

The sledges came down very fast. No one tried to walk up the path. The runners of the sledges polished the snow smooth. The path had a cover of glass. The long sledges manned by four, five people were the fastest. They descended straight from the top to the bottom of Calvary Hill without skidding to the right or left. They raced on over the level ground. They stopped far away from Calvary Hill – behind the hospital entrance. The nuns and the orphanage children had reached the top.

One boy lay down on a sledge on his stomach, holding on to the runners. Three others sat on his back. Three drivers with four heads, eight legs raced downhill. Two sledges were loaded up one behind the other. A boy on the rear sledge held on to the one in front. Both sledges – linked by his arms – slithered down.

— That's too dangerous. Don't even try to do it once. If you're thrown from the slide, if you fall, arms and legs will get broken. Your head could be torn off by the impact.

One boy lay on his stomach on a short, light sledge. He steered with his feet. The sledge spun round, swung from side to side, jumped.

Thick roots grew across the path, out of the wood. The sledges grazed them. They veered off the path, rolled over, tumbled across the slope. The runners struck the pedestals of the plaques of the Passion.

— The enemy aircraft tumble out of the clouds when they're shot down.

At the top, at the starting point, the nuns jumped in the way, if too many orphanage children wanted to get on one sledge. They braced themselves against the runners. They pulled the children back by their clothes. They pushed the sledges to the start.

Something cracked under Detlev. The battens pressed against his legs. The wind forced the water out of his eyes. The wind caught his face, smacked against his ears.

Detlev held on tightly to the bars of the sledge as he thundered over the tree roots.

He recognized nothing on the plaques, no yellow haloes, no brown beard, no pink mantle. A boy slid off. The sledge overturned, slid upside down into a tree – the white wood under the bark flashed out. The others steered round the boy who had fallen off. Sledges turned at right angles. Boys struck their heads against wood, against ice, against iron. One limped, one bled, one hopped from one foot to the other, two were crying. At the top the other sledges were stopped. Some children slid down on foot. When they stood up thick patches of snow were sticking to their clothes. As

they moved, the white patches fell apart into little flecks. The
sledges were pulled to the side. The slide was free again.

— If something had happened.

If the iron runners had gone straight over a leg, over a wrist,
had rattled over his neck, had struck the head of an orphanage child who didn't get out of the way in time. Bones would
have been broken in pieces. Blood would have trickled onto
the snow. The torn-off limbs would have been taken away.
Only a red spot would have been left on the slide. It was
Detlev's turn to pull the sledge up the hill.

Two skiers came skimming along the crest of the line of
hills.

— 'The heritage of Björndal' – 'And forever sing the forests.'
That's not for you.

In Steingriff the boys made their own skis. They sawed off
planks. The tips were cut from plywood and bent into shape
over steam. Towards evening, steam enveloped Calvary Hill.

— This is the last time. Whoever starts now, should just stay
at the bottom.

Someone took the sledge away from Detlev. Detlev watched
the two skiers.

Detlev remembered Sepp's father, who came home from the
munitions factory in the middle of the night in winter. Sepp's
father's jacket was cold to the touch. Detlev had imagined
that black air would waft out of the jacket if one shook it.

Sometimes Sepp's father brought crumbled chocolate home
with him, Brown chocolate. Not white.

— There's something special in it. To keep you awake. Our
brave pilots are given it to revive them when they're in action
against the enemy.

The two skiers left four even tracks in the snow. They didn't
race downhill like the orphanage children. They skied along
the highest ridge of the line of hills. They pushed the rods
with the little wheels into the snow on either side, drew them
out again, pierced the snow with them once more. Had there

been a fifth track in the snow, Detlev would have been able
to mark out a treble clef across the five lines in the snow with
his feet.

— A man with one leg doesn't ski.

The dots made by the rods would have looked like notes and
a giant man with a recorder like a tree trunk would play a song
behind the two skiers and blow them before him.

The two skiers grew smaller and blacker. Without visible
movements they pushed themselves towards the next copse.
Detlev stood at the top of the hill. Below him the orphanage children were shouting at one another, as they went
down. The nuns fluttered down between the pictures of
the Passion. The other boys from the town, the boys from
the villages had gone home.

Detlev hopped, slipped over the smooth polished tree roots.
He bumped into the trees and the plaques with outstretched
arms.

The nuns hadn't noticed his absence. They were astonished
when he came.

— There would be no snow. Now there's no snow anyway. Even
in winter there would be no snow any more. There would be
no winter at all. What is snow? What would there not be? The
ashes of mummy's friend in the urn would not be among the
ashes of the burned house. In winter ashes are needed for
gritting. Snow is nothing. Snow is white. When it warms
up, it melts. Only transparent water is left. Nothing remains
of the white colours, no chalk, no flour, no light grey ashes.
Snow doesn't smell of anything. Snow smells of something
that nothing else smells of. Snow smells of glass or of the air
in the jacket of Sepp's father or of the air in grandad's jacket,
when he comes back into the cellar.

— It's burning in the east.

— Everything's calm now.

— It won't be bad this time.

— I can hear the sound of aircraft to the northwest.

— Snow is nothing. There would be no snow.

By the next lesson he could play the song perfectly. Mother
Cecilia had taken him down to the big hall too early.
— They're still rehearsing the third scene of the second act.
On the platform, dust was whirling up into the air. A man
with a white elephant's foot was bending over another man
whose face was bandaged.
— I am King Herod, what I say, shall be done. You lie,
master astrologer. I shall have you thrown to the rats in the
tower forthwith.
The tower had trembled from the howling of the sirens.
The nun with the glasses called out:
— I can't hear the un of 'shall be done'. When you say 'tower'
we must be able to hear the E and the R at the end. Otherwise
it was good. Go and get your food. Now Detlev can play his
song.
Detlev stood on the platform with his legs apart. King Herod
and the astrologer went away. He wasn't King Herod. He
was no astrologer. They were wearing pyjama trousers with
field grey coats over them. They had spoken like the astrologer and the king. Alfred and Odel and Joachim-Devil had
screamed as if they really were three devils. The orphanage
children had played at mass, while Detlev had been with his
mother in the veterinary surgeon's house. The orphanage
children had spoken hoarsely like the short parish priest.
They had sung and spoken in Latin. They made the sign
of the cross like the bishop, who tripped as he walked. They
shouted like the tall pale priest. They couldn't understand
the strange language. They pattered off the litany by heart.
At first Detlev could not speak Bavarian. Now he can't
speak anything else any more. Grandfather, grandmother,
Aunt Hilde and Uncle Emil will not understand him. They
already couldn't understand him the last time, when he was

on holiday in Hamburg with his mother. The two wounded soldiers spoke like King Herod and like the astrologer. They weren't even wearing astrologers' clothes and kings' clothes. Detlev didn't make any mistakes. Detlev, alone, on the middle of the platform.

— Go onto the stage.

— That's the stage.

— During rehearsals no one is allowed on the stage.

— Come down from the stage again now.

Planks across beer barrels – like at the 'Romantic Evenings' at the Post Inn. Right and left, above, below, electric light bulbs burned in oblong boxes. It was dark in the hall.

He played 'O little children come' without mistakes.

Detlev didn't looked around. Perhaps they were all sitting behind him, were looking at him from behind: The wounded soldiers with elephant feet and big wings and bridges of wire and plaster. They were sitting on rails, crouching in cages, without ears, deaf, on artificial rocks of concrete or papier maché – the three devils, the three kings, King Herod, Franz, Mrs Weindeln, all the orphanage children in little priests' and bishops' vestments.

— No bomb will ever fall on Hagenbeck's Zoo.

— After Klasel has been, we'll all move down to the dormitory. Then the dining room upstairs will be made ready for the distribution of presents and for our own Christmas play. Ours is much nicer than the one with the wounded. Only the real orphans are allowed to take part in our Christmas play. In Hamburg there was no Klasel. At first Detlev didn't even understand the word. Now when he thinks back to the white tulle cloth, he doesn't know how to spell the name. He would be unable to put it together on the lid of the letter case.

The first time in Steingriff:

— Klasel is coming soon.

— Klasel is coming tomorrow.

— Klasel is coming today.

In the mornings the sky was dark blue with a red spot over the forest. The lorries were leaving the saw mill. Behind the wheels of the trailer sat a man wearing motor cycle goggles and overalls.

— Klasel looks something like that. But that's not Klasel.

— What does the man behind the wheels do?

— He brakes when the trees are loaded.

The chains for the tree trunks jangled across the snow encrusted asphalt.

— That's how Klasel jangles his chains.

Sledges with ringing bells drove out of the farmyard gates.

— That could be Klasel, making his enquiries.

— Perhaps it's Klasel's wife. That would be a bad sign.

The word 'Klas' is only an abbreviation for Saint Nicholas or Father Christmas, it's one and the same thing. Klasel brings children apples and nuts and toys in his sack. Or should do. I wonder what he can bring now there's a war on. – For the bad boys there'll be a couple of strokes of the rod. His mother stopped talking because of an unspoken word.

— There's still something on the tip of your tongue.

— You're a nosey parker.

His mother was silent again.

— She'll say something straightaway so that I don't think she's keeping something secret.

— Klasel has already been to ask me whether you've been good too. He asks everyone in the village. So he had to ask me too.

— Was I good?

— You were good. You have to be good. You have to be far too good. You see how many wounded there are. So many things can happen to one and much worse things than being shot dead.

— What's worse than being shot dead?

— Being tortured. You don't need to be afraid of Klasel. I told him what a bright and intelligent boy you are, that you always obey your mother and do your school work neatly. I would rather not have said it, what's the point of making children frightened of a bogeyman at a time like this. Don't worry. You'll see.

In Hamburg no Saint Nicholas ran from water tower to water tower on winter nights, from Windsbergen to the zoo, from Niendorf Wood to the Alster.

Once a lovely red Father Christmas with a cotton wool beard stood on the Jungfernstieg and nodded. Grandmother squeezed Detlev's hand. She was taking him to buy a box of building bricks.

Perhaps there had been a Nicholas in the hospital, when Detlev had been admitted with measles. Perhaps Saint Nicholas had brought the grocery shop and the other box of building bricks.

Later no lights were allowed on the streets in the evening any more. There were no Christmas trees with electric candles on the Jungfernstieg any more. There was no red Father Christmas any more. There was no grocery shop any more.

— There would have been no grocery shop at all.

There was no toy sewing machine any more. Grandfather let down the blackout blinds on all the windows. His mother no longer brought any brown or any white chocolate home from the shop in the evening. Twice a little red boot full of nuts, and with a fir twig, a few strips of lametta, stood in the dark. It still wasn't Christmas. Then it wasn't long till Christmas any more.*

He tapped at the window first. The two girls, Sepp, Sepp's parents, his mother, Detlev quickly ran into the warm kitchen. Sepp's parents hugged their children tightly.

*Saint Nicholas brings small presents on December 6th.

Detlev's mother looked round the kitchen. No one sat down on a chair. No one placed an apple on the stove plate. Sepp wasn't sawing at anything with his fretsaw. Everyone stood close together in a corner of the kitchen, opposite the door, far away from the door.

— How sore is it, if you're tortured? Mummy had no idea, otherwise she would have done it differently.

It sounded as if Klasel was as big as the elephant on the chain in the elephant house. He scraped along against both walls of the passageway, he clattered over the flagstones, he knocked against the ceiling of the passageway. There was a hammering on the outside door, then he was already knocking on the kitchen door. Sepp and his sisters began to cry.

— In the hay loft he pretends to be so brave.

Detlev didn't want to cry.

Klasel threw open the door. Now Detlev couldn't cry any more. Behind his forehead everything tightened – around his eyes everything became dry and hard. Detlev would have liked to have turned round and jumped through the wall.

Klasel had no eyes, no nose, no mouth. His face was made of a flat, cheesy, flapping mass of meat. In place of eyes he had small bulges without any eye white, without pupils, without lids, without lashes.

Unlike the death's head on the soldiers' caps he didn't have any big holes in place of the nose. His nose was a small bulge without nostrils. He had no ears. Instead of hands, black clumps without fingers, without finger nails, without hair on the fingers stuck out of the sleeves. He held a sack in the two clumps. An iron pigtail grew from his head.

— He has to cut the others' fingers off and the ears and the nose. He has to poke out the eyes of those who have been naughty and pull out their finger nails.

Klasel took a step into the kitchen. He had no eyes, he didn't see the start of the linoleum. He fell over like a crane. Klasel with the cheese head lay at Detlev's feet.

Detlev's mother took him by the hand and walked out of the door.

When it grew dark, Detlev didn't let his mother leave him alone any more. Detlev began to scream. Detlev was afraid that Klasel could be hiding behind the windows, under the bed, in the stove. In the evening Detlev no longer dared to stand by the door. In the morning, in the dark, he was afraid if he had to walk to the road alone, where he met the other children. In the morning his fear was not so great. The night was ending. The darkness was no longer growing thicker and thicker, but was gradually turning into the white light of day. Even during the day Detlev was afraid of the vent hole of the cellar and of the lavatory hole. Klasel could have popped up out of the toilet with his white face that looked like the flesh on the legs of Sepp's father.

His mother said:

— Klasel wasn't a Klasel. It was the farm labourer from next door. He had a cow bell and chain from the well. The milking cloth was hanging over his face. Don't be so afraid, be a brave boy. You must have seen that it was an old piece of curtain material.

Sepp said:

— Klasel's wife is even more dangerous than Klasel himself. She only comes once every four years. She's seven times as bad. Sometimes she comes unexpectedly. One day after – one day before her husband. She's black all over. She has one red and one green eye. At night you can already see her eyes gleaming in the distance. But then it's too late. She always sees you first. She finds someone wherever they're hiding. She catches everyone she wants to get. She beats the bad children, the good ones get no reward from her. Often she takes some with her. They have to work for her. Plaiting birches and sorting bones, making whips. She doesn't give the children anything to eat. They nibble at themselves with hunger. They eat the hair off their own heads. And hair is poisonous. If one of them doesn't obey, she pulls out his toe nails or finger nails with pliers. The worst thing is, you never know exactly when she's going to come and into which houses she'll go and who she'll take away with her. A few years ago she took three away with her from the main road one morning. We had expected her this year. She'll definitely come next year. On horseback. She rides.

The orphanage children said:

— Klasel is coming tomorrow.

They were happy. First they were bathed in pairs in a tub – with a cloth around their hips – by Sister Appia.

Detlev made himself very small. He drew up his shoulders. He hunched his back. He drew in his head – when the nuns came running from the windows crying:

— We've seen him down on the church square. He's coming. He's coming.

— Mother hasn't come yet.

Detlev looked down at the floor. When he heard Klasel knocking at the door, he shut his eyes tight. But behind his lids waited the Klasel from Steingriff with the face without eyes, falling towards him. Klasel's wife rode by. Detlev saw Steingriff in spring. The cows were brought to the meadow, radishes sown, potatoes planted. The farmers were afraid of the winter, because Klasel's wife would come then. The grain ripened. The school classes ran into the wood. The children picked blueberries, chanterelles. They didn't laugh. They didn't sing. In winter no one dared go out into the street any more. No light burned behind the windows. The chimneys didn't smoke.

Detlev let some light between his eyelids. He wanted to press them together again right away. He hoped that the village of Steingriff and Klasel and the horse and Klasel's wife would be destroyed by the short interruption and that the new Klasel from the orphanage couldn't fall in through the tiny slit.

Detlev saw the new Klasel. The old one disappeared. Detlev
opened his eyes wide.

The new one, who sat on a high throne in front of the orphanage children, really was the Saint Nicholas his mother and
Sister Silissa had talked about. He looked like God in the
town hall chamber under whom the gauleiter had been laid
out. Saint Nicholas wore a cotton wool beard like the Father
Christmas by the Alster in Hamburg. His cheeks were pink.
He had brown eyes with white lids. He had a snub-nose, a
small, pale mouth and protruding ears. He was wrapped in
a loose red cloak. The pointed, gilded cap on his head was
shaking. Two angels were busy beside him, threatening with
little golden rods and pulling presents out of a sack. Each
orphanage child was called out by name.

— Saint Nicholas knows everything.

— Alfred, this year you have been a kindhearted person.

— Erwin, you must work harder at school.

— Rosi should help more in the kitchen.

— Anna, our problem child.

No one was thrashed with the rods. Only for Joachim-Devil
did the two angels point the rods at Saint Nicholas.

— Joachim, you are causing the dedicated sisters a great
deal of sorrow because of your incurable wickedness. Really
I shouldn't give you a present at all, but should chastise you
with a hard rod. Are you going to better yourself at last,
Joachim, so that your comrades no longer need to give you
the nickname 'Devil'?

— Yes, I want to better myself, dear holy Saint Nicholas.

— Then today we shall allow mercy precedence over justice
and put away the rods for the last time and allow even you to
receive a small present.

— God bless you, dear holy Saint Nicholas.

— Now comes a little musician.

The floor boards under Detlev grew longer. He saw the
beard, the white eyelids of Saint Nicholas grow larger and

the recorder in Sister Appia's hand grow larger. He took the recorder, placed it between his lips, pushed the halting breath out of his mouth into the plastic tube with holes, raised his fingers pressed them down. He didn't look at the recorder, not at his fidgeting fingers. Detlev looked at Saint Nicholas's face. Detlev waited for the moment when the pink Saint Nicholas would tear off his lovable face, and below it would appear the other one, white, made of cheese, of the flesh on Sepp's father's calves – without eyes and ears, with warts in the place of eyes and a scab in the place of the mouth.

— Why are you looking at Saint Nicholas so angrily? You don't need to be afraid. You are an obedient and musical boy. You pray with great fervour and though you're a Protestant you even go regularly go Holy Mass. Keep on like this and everything will turn out well.

— Perhaps he really is our heavenly Father? No. Our heavenly Father doesn't have a woman's voice.

Detlev was allowed to go down to the big hall alone – without Mother Cecilia. He played the song. The nun with the glasses turned the pages in the book. Sister Augusta smiled at the doll. The other nun crossed the stage with the cardboard pitcher on her head.

The orphanage which Detlev was beginning to know, whose stairs were growing smaller, whose ceilings were getting lower, whose rooms were contracting, the orphanage he had known was turning into another orphanage. The nuns cut it in half, they shook the rooms and jumbled them up. No one was allowed into the dining room. The Christ Child was to be allowed to fly in and out undisturbed. The Christmas play had to be rehearsed up there. Only Joachim-Devil was allowed up. He had a part.

— He's playing the devil.

— I'm not playing the devil at all. I'm playing Leander who gets lost in the wood.

— I hope you drop dead in the wood.

— Drop dead yourself.

— 'Yes, dear holy Saint Nicholas. Very good, dear holy Saint Nicholas.' Anyway, holy and saint are one and the same thing. Didn't you notice how sensibly even Detlev behaved? Did you all hear: Here comes a little musician. If you go into the dining room, the Christ Child will fly right out again.

Sister Appia and Erwin carried the dining tables down to the dormitory. They ate beside the beds.

— Like robbers.

— 'At six in the morn, we went on our way.'

— '. . .had to pay.'

— '. . .were done away.'

— If the Christ Child hears things like that through the ceiling.

The strips of moonlight across the dormitory were differently indented from usual, when Detlev woke up in the middle of the night, held his breath and swallowed down his saliva, listened. The strips of moonlight mounted over shoes, benches, tables, coats, bed rails.

— Joachim-Devil has been chosen to take part in the play again this year. He doesn't grow fat out of pure badness. He farts. But he's just perfect for acting in the Christmas play. Last year he had to weep by a spring. Everyone wept with him. Even the parish priest. And how happy he was with the bread that came from the Christ Child himself. In reality it wasn't bread, only painted cardboard lids, the nuns keep them in a box all year and take them out for the Christmas play. In peace time they use real bread for the performances. Every year the nuns read through hundreds of books and only then do they decide what is to be performed. Joachim-Devil has to learn a whole book by heart. He's best at remembering the sentences, that's why they take him again and again. But after all the most difficult thing remains the choice and then all the things that have to be decided: What should the actors

wear? Where should the light fall? The curtain ropes have
to be fastened somewhere in the dining room. The artificial
bushes for the countryside have to be procured and the chairs
and the hall clock and the door for the room of the poor
craftsman and his family and the delicate heavenly tinkling
when the Christ Child appears on stage.
— You're mad. It's not as bad as that. But the hall has to
be scrubbed, that's why they throw us out. The fir tree
is screwed into its base. It comes at night, it's pulled up
over the balcony, so that no one sees it beforehand. It's ten
feet tall. It always hides the cross completely – because it's
Christmas. Christ nailed to the cross isn't right then. The fir
tree is wonderful to look at. There's nothing more beautiful in
the world. It's only another two weeks, then we'll be allowed
up again.
First the giving of presents at his mother's:
The new room was in the attic. The backs of the unlined roof
tiles looked like the raw muscles of a rabbit, when grandfather
skinned it in front of the allotment house.
Detlev had to wait outside until his mother rang a bell. The fir
tree was very small. It stood in a flower pot. Coloured figures
from the Winter Relief Fund dangled above the candles.
The reddish light over the hair, the face, the hands of his
mother, over the suitcases in the corner, over the table with
the little packages and letters and sweets was, for Detlev, the
most beautiful light he had ever seen. He liked it better than
the yellow light in summer, than the orange red at sunrise and
sunset, than the thick, milky light between the hop poles. He
didn't need to be afraid of the almost motionless light, as he
was of the flickering flames of the candles in the church tower,
of the moonlight and the light of the stars which sent a cold
shudder down his back.
Detlev's mother cried at his happiness. Then Detlev cried
because his mother was crying. Then they both laughed,
because they had cried – instead of laughing.

— There are other reasons for crying. We're almost at peace here. At any rate we're not at the front. We're together.

— Is my father at the front?

— No. Let's just talk about nice things. We should really think about the fallen.

Detlev sees Sepp's father falling over outside the munitions factory. He sees a white field. Alfred, Frieda, Shaky, Rosi, Siegfried, Siegfried's father step out of the wood. They cross the white field. They fall over. The white is stained red. Captains come from every side and collect the heads, the legs, the pouches, the medals, the caps, the edelweiss and the gentian in big coffins. The captains come without black horses. They pass by without turning to look at the bloody heap. The captains don't come. The hands and feet are left lying in the snow.

Fathers come running over the white field. First their heads are broken. Holes are shot in their stomachs. The blood runs into the snow. They fall over and don't move.

— I got cross about the chemist. I was paying him the money for next month. He was complaining about women who wipe their babies' bottoms with cotton wool.

— In war time, cotton wool is needed for the wounded.

— No one's denying that. But there are babies who have got chafed from lying or they have such sensitive skin that one can only wipe them clean with cotton wool. You know just as little about that as the chemist.

— Joachim-Devil never uses newspaper. He always uses his finger. He wipes his finger against the wall.

— What a thing to talk about on Christmas Eve.

A semolina cake from grandmother. A letter from grandmother and grandfather in Gothic and Latin script. Two pairs of long socks from grandmother. A Rübezahl figure from the Giant Mountains from grandfather. If Detlev held the table at an angle, the Rübezahl figure began to run by itself. Two two-mark coins with President Hindenburg.

Detlev's mother gave him a cap with ear flaps.

— In case it gets as cold again as last winter.

Detlev's mother gave him a new recorder book and five cellophane pictures and a farm with a farmer's wife, a farmer, two cows, a cart, two trees. The farm house could be folded up. His mother had made marzipan potatoes out of semolina and butter and almond flavouring.

When Detlev and his mother walked across the church square, the package with the presents bumped against Detlev's legs.

— Detlev's got a Russian hat on.

— Detlev's got a Russian hat.

His mother stayed with him. The orphanage children assembled downstairs in the hall. His mother leant against the wall beside Sister Appia. Detlev didn't look over to her. Alfred came and stood beside Detlev and tugged at the package with the presents.

Everyone went out. Detlev felt as if the darkness with all its stars was falling onto the back of his neck.

Half of the houses, of the church was gone. Only the walls of houses still stood in Scheyern. The snow-covered roofs were like the ground. The windows were tied shut. Water didn't gush from Saint Joseph's Fountain any more.

— In winter the town saves the money for the mountain water.

A shutter sealed off the windows of the devotional articles shop. The arcade was dark.

— In winter you can save the money for ice cream. You can put snow in your mouth. It doesn't taste of anything. But it's as cold as vanilla ice. Snow doesn't even taste of water.

The blackout was complete.

— Scheyern hasn't been bombed yet. But they're afraid. They could be punished too. That's why they keep to the blackout regulations.

The market square would rock back and forwards. Brown
earth would spout up from below the snow. The houses
would topple over.

Through the blackout paper Detlev heard little bells, Christmas songs, radio music.

— I wanted to be an actress when I was younger, his mother
said to Sister Appia.

Mother Cecilia led Detlev away from the orphanage children
and his mother. She took charge of the package. She pulled
him through many doors, through dark rooms, down unlit
stairs. She pushed him into a shadowy room.

— Wait here.

Someone gripped Detlev's hand. Something jingled.

— Don't scream or anything. Don't you recognize me?

Detlev recognized a foot in plaster on the floor in front of him.
A red coat fell onto the white foot. The red material reached
up to the shoulders of the wounded soldier. The man's face
smelt of cake shops, of his mother's little box, in the house
with the cockerel foot soup.

— In 'The Crib' there was almond pudding with raspberry
sauce. Mummy didn't promise me anything that wasn't true.
In the orphanage there was never almond pudding with raspberry sauce.

The face of the wounded soldier came closer. It became
round. The nose stood out. The eye sockets receded. The
ears grew out to the right and the left. The Adam's apple
began to move. Smoke mixed with the smell of his mother's
little box. A spot glowed and shone under the nose of the
wounded soldier. The cheeks became bright red. The lips
blood red. The lids blue. The eye lashes grew longer. The
hair became as yellow as clay.

— Don't you recognize me?

— No. Yes.

— I'm one of the three kings. There's some surprises in store
for you.

The walls gradually receded. Violet light shone from bulbs which had been arranged in a square round a curtain.

— They're sitting behind that.

— Who?

— Everyone.

— Who?

— The town council. The heavenly girls. The police. The people from the Party. And the rest of my comrades.

— And everyone from the orphanage and my mummy as well?

— This is the stage. It's about to start.

All the men were wearing long skirts. Some limped. They carried little boxes and spears. They were brightly painted and had furrowed faces. The Virgin Mary's lips turned black in the violet light. The blue tint of her eyelids looked like leaves of larkspur. She too had many wrinkles around her nose, around her eyes, around her mouth. A wounded soldier made up as a negro smoked a pipe.

The Virgin Mary lifted Detlev up and carried him over to a small hole in the curtain. Everything was bright on the other side. Every chair was taken. The whole hall was full of people. The wounded rested the wire frames and the boards with the plaster wings on the backs of chairs. Two nuns carried in half a man.

— He looks like a lizard that's lost its tail.

— Don't talk such nonsense, otherwise I'll let you fall.

At the back the other soldiers were crowding in on their crutches. They wanted to move more quickly than the two nuns with the half man.

The nuns set him down in a soft armchair and stuffed soft cushions under his hips – where his body ended. The soldiers with the crutches swung their fat plaster legs back and forward until they had found a good place. They sank down onto the chairs. The nuns wagged their fingers, when the wounded made too much noise with their crutches. Detlev wanted to wave to his mother. She was sitting right under him.

— There's no point in doing that. You can wave your arms about as much as you like. She can't see you from down there. Now you've seen enough. I can't hold you any longer.

Mother Cecilia fetched him away. She led Detlev into a room full of clothes, swords, baskets, mirrors. The wounded were sitting around in their underwear. They had a lot of hair on their legs. The hairdresser – five combs in his pocket – was rubbing brown paint into their faces. When it was Detlev's turn, his face was painted with make-up too. The hairdresser painted rings around his eyes with his pencil. Detlev was powdered – like a baby between the legs – Detlev's face was covered with white powder.

Under the violet curtains:

The lions were roaring across from Hagenbeck's Zoo. It was six. They were being fed. Powder and Nivea cream were mixed up together on the couch cover. His mother's make-up pencils lay in the little black box.

Mother Cecilia pulled a pair of yellow trousers and a small green jacket onto him. She hung a loose cloak around his shoulders. He had no time to look in the mirror.

— Out of here. The space is needed for others.

Mother Cecilia led Detlev back into the violet lit room.

— The shepherd boy. A shepherd boy. What a fine-looking shepherd boy. Where did you pick him up?

— It's Detlev.

— We don't believe that.

— Yes. I am Detlev.

— And I suppose I'm the parish priest.

The nuns clapped their hands. The nuns pushed the wounded soldiers. They held forefinger to mouth.

— The priest dresses up. His mother dresses up. Alfred and the others dressed up as priests. Sister Augusta dresses up as the Virgin Mary. The consecration, what does that mean? The consecration happens at the altar. Alfred, Odel, Joachim-Devil were devils. Siegfried was brave and not a coward like Siegfried.

The curtain was gathered together on both sides. A large black barn appeared behind it. There was coughing and sneezing on the floor of the barn. Mother Cecilia said to Detlev:

— You can't go up yet. The shepherds have to receive the good tidings first. Keep still. You mustn't make a mistake when you play. When you've finished the song you must remain sitting and look happily in front of you, till the curtain sweeps shut again. Because it's a tableau vivant.

The two sides of the curtain unfolded again and drew shut in the middle. The tins of the three wise kings rattled. The Virgin Mary's blue dress rustled. The doll baby fell to the floor. A bench, straw, a manger were carried onto the stage. The Virgin Mary took the doll baby onto her lap.

— Mary didn't have any cotton wool in the stall. Our Lord Jesus Christ's skin must have been very sensitive when he was small. There was only straw.

The curtain in front of Detlev disappeared. Light shone from all sides. The light lifted the people on the stage up – in a single movement – just as the tall pale priest lifted up the monstrance.

The dark auditorium looked like his grandmother's square button box. One grey, two-holed button above the other. The buttons only varied in size. Not even the half man could be made out. Detlev looked in vain for his mother in the audience.

The Christ Child smiled up at his mother. Detlev played 'O little children come'.

Detlev tried to follow each note of his recorder as it threaded the button holes in the black barn right to the very last row. Detlev played without a mistake. If he had made a mistake, he would have fallen from the narrow, shining sickle on which he travelled through the night with the Virgin Mary and the Christ Child and the water carrier.

The thread would have broken. The buttons would have tumbled noisily on top of one another.

The Virgin Mary smiled at Detlev. The three kings entered and laid down the presents for the Christ Child beside Detlev.

A light was switched on right at the back of the box. At the rear wall of the hall a group of wounded soldiers stood up. They weren't wearing bandages, but had crutches. As Detlev held the last note, he saw the clear syrupy drops falling onto the wounds from dead Marie's tubes. He saw the nuns' fingers pressing the edges of the wounds together, as the boys in Steingriff pressed the edges and flaps of the model aeroplanes together.

The wounded held sheets of music in their hands. A small black man jumped around in front of the light. He raised his arms, waved, trembled. As deep as the siren before it stopped gurgling, the wounded soldiers sang, 'A rose it has blossomed.'

The Virgin Mary hummed along.

The curtain stretched across the box again. Wounded soldiers pulled the straw, the crib, the bench to the side, took the Christ Child away from Sister Augusta, tilted columns in, made up a bed. Herod with his crown lay down on the bed. The box opened again. The stage was not yet quite lit up, as Herod began to groan. A white cross was dancing about on the stage. Herod screamed:

— Not on me. Not on me.

He held his ears with pain. He stuck his head in his own arm-pit.

Detlev ran away. Mother Cecilia behind him.

— Why is the king screaming so terribly? Did you see the white cross? It was a ghost. Or the Christ Child. The Christ Child is angry. Was it the devil, coming to fetch Herod?

— But it was only the beam of light from our projector. We do it like that every year.

— But that means the Christ Child. Why is the Christ Child so angry and torturing King Herod so terribly?

— Because Herod had all the little children killed.

— Mother Cecilia, King Herod is screaming so terribly.

On the way back Erwin screamed:

— Not on me. Not on me.

His mother had gone back to her room.

— You played very well, Detlev.

—The beam of light is the Christ Child. The devil has possessed the three of them. The beam of light falls on King Herod like the devil on Alfred, Odel and Joachim-Devil. Because of the beam of light Herod falls into a fit like Anna. The beam of light falls onto Sister Augusta, the doll baby becomes the Christ Child.

— What kind of make-up did you put on?

— We have paint like that in the orphanage as well for our Christmas play.

— How do you get the make-up off again?

— Afterwards the hairdresser comes and rubs brillantine on your face and wipes it all off with toilet paper.

— Were you proud when you were allowed to play?

Joachim-Devil played a poor, starving boy. He often had to speak alone and for a long time. On the stage in the orphanage – it wasn't a stage, the floor went from the audience over to Joachim-Devil without rising – over there – on the other side – behind the wire on which the two curtains were hung – Joachim-Devil spoke like a devout boy. Anna held her head to the side and looked up, but she didn't fall from her chair. Alfred bit his fingers out of fear that Joachim-Devil could forget his lines. Sister Silissa quietly spoke every word that Joachim-Devil spoke, along with him. Mother Superior wept. He wasn't as beautifully dressed as the wounded in the hospital. He had no make-up on his face. Throughout the whole piece Detlev could recognize that it was Joachim-Devil. Detlev cried, as Joachim-Devil cried with hunger in the bushes in the dining room. When he took his bow, as all the orphanage children were clapping with the priest and the nuns, Joachim-Devil was red in the face, like a real devil.

The presents were distributed:

Detlev received a book. In red Gothic letters on the grey cover stood: Children's Schott.

There were many drawings in the book. Under the drawings Detlev read:

The young believer at prayer.

The young believer in the drawing had an asparagus head, no cheeks, three hairs, a body like a Christmas biscuit.

The young believer at Holy Communion. The young believer with folded hands. The young believer with closed eyes. The young believer with eyes raised upwards. The young believer drinking from the communion cup. The young believer kneeling. Detlev had turned the pages of the book.

The Christmas tree completely concealed the blue-white, bent, bloodstained Christ. The tip of the fir tree was bent over under the ceiling. Several thick silver baubles hung on every twig. Angel hair hung from the branches like straw from the fork in Steingriff.

When Detlev had wished for the box of building bricks in Hamburg, he saw a fir tree, silver, like the Christmas tree in the orphanage, in the toy catalogue. It was a fir tree made of Meccano parts. Screws held the metal bar branches together – instead of needles the fir tree had holes.

— Now my mother is coming across the church square below.

At Easter Detlev counted it off on his fingers. The fingers moved once more. One, two, three, four. The Christ Child on Sister Augusta's arm changed into a man with a beard, whom the sacristan pushed between the cardboard rocks in front of the altar.

— There wouldn't be the month of January, the month of February, the month of March. There wouldn't be a birthday.

— In Bavaria we don't celebrate birthdays. Catholics celebrate name days.

There remain the dolls and the sacristan's son's sugar lamb. Detlev sees the dolls. They grow larger before his eyes. A doll's eye fills his vision.

— The doll's eye was not a doll's eye.

Alfred, Odel, Siegfried, Erwin, Joachim-Devil, little Xaver, didn't try to do anything to Detlev any more. They were friendlier to him. But Detlev didn't notice. Detlev thought only of the journey to Hamburg. His happiness at the departure was like the taste of a bedtime sweet which Sister Silissa slipped him in the evening before going to sleep, and which he quickly put in his mouth along with the paper, so that the others didn't notice and become envious.

Between Christmas and Easter Erwin screamed – whenever he met Detlev in a dark corner:

— Not on me. Not on me.

Detlev turns his head, looks down from the balcony. He sees himself turning his head, as all the orphanage children looked down from the balcony.

The nuns had laid two hens' eggs dyed brown with onion skins on the dining tables for each child.

Detlev knew that both he and little Xaver would look for proper Easter eggs once more with their mothers. The sacristan's son ran through the church yard below. He held the bushes with their fresh leaves aside. Behind the holly tree he squealed with pleasure. He held up a pink animal with a red ribbon round its neck. From above, the orphanage children saw the laughter in the face of the sacristan's son. But the orphanage children couldn't tell what kind of animal

it was. The sacristan's son pressed it to himself. He ran – his cheek against the animal's body – to his parents. He turned in a circle with the animal. He rocked it. When the sacristan's son noticed that all the orphanage children were leaning over the top of the balcony railing and following his movements with their heads, he held the animal high above his head.
— It's the Easter Lamb, of course.
— What else could it have been?
A small golden bell hung from the red ribbon. The orphanage children stood up straight again.
— Don't lean so greedily over the railing.
— They're happy because none of them has received a pink lamb.
— We shouldn't grudge him it. It's the Lamb of Christ. The Agnus Dei. It's made of sugar. He deserved something nice.
His mother came through the dining room, stepped onto the balcony, took him by the hand.
— Mummy is about to come through the dining room, step onto the balcony and take me by the hand.
The procession came closer. The cross swayed above the praying people.
— In the hazel bush I too was ready to be nailed to the cross for Our Lord Jesus Christ.
Frieda asked him:
— Do you want to backslide.
Detlev thought:
— I want to backslide.
Christmas was long past. In the dining room the only remaining decoration was the cross, the first thing he had seen when he entered the room for the first time. It was Easter again.
At the church entrance the procession divided into two groups. The man who was carrying the cross, struck the door with the upper end of the longtitudinal beam. One group sang a verse in Latin. The other group replied singing.

The priests sang behind the closed doors. At Easter there were three priests. They ran around the altar, carried thick books, swung censers, swung sprinklers of holy water, lifted up hosts. They bumped into one another. They made mistakes in their singing. They got the movements mixed up.

In the church the sacristan had constructed Our Lord's tomb out of cardboard and supports. One of the three priests gave a sign at a certain point – or the sacristan knew when without a sign. He turned a handle behind the rock pushing forward a carved Christ figure with a red and golden flag in its hand.

Joachim-Devil had already explained this surprise to Detlev in advance, so that Detlev wouldn't be so frightened again as at the death of King Herod, so that Detlev didn't start to scream as at the appearance of the three devils.

Detlev woke up.

— I have to pee.

There was a new moon.

— Why does one say new moon when there's no moon in the sky at all?

It was so dark that the breathing of the sleepers sounded quieter than usual to Detlev.

— I must get up, otherwise I'll do it in the bed.

He sat up. He held his breath. He swallowed down saliva. He listened, to hear whether one of the others would interrupt their regular breathing because of his movement, would swallow down saliva.

Nothing changed.

Detlev put his feet on the floor. He waited, in case anyone grabbed his ankles from under the bed. No one grabbed him. He took the first step. His feet made a smacking noise on the linoleum. The linoleum ended. Detlev had found the doorway without first groping to the right and to the left with his hands.

The smell changed. There was no longer a smell of urine. There was a smell of soda. Where there began to be a smell of burnt fat, Detlev turned to the right. He stretched out his hands in front of him. He bumped against the iron flower stand in the hall. He felt the threshhold under his feet. He went further. The tiles in the little passageway were warmer and not as smooth as the tiles in the hall. The lavatories were on the right. There was a smell of cold turd. Detlev sat down on the hole in the wooden board.

— If you're afraid and if you're shivering, you can't. I haven't got any paper. I would have to wipe myself with my hands. I only need to pee. Does the Lord God have to go to the lavatory? I mustn't think that, otherwise I'll go to hell.

Detlev stood up. The lavatory door. The warmer tiles. The smell of geraniums.

Detlev bumped against the stairs. Detlev felt his way along the wall till he came to the door. He went in. It grew warmer. It smelled of warm, wet cloths. A clock ticked in the warmth. Detlev opened the next door. Behind it was the church square. Outside it was brighter. Detlev pushed the door shut. There was a bang.

— Who's coming now?

Detlev continued to feel his way. He bumped against the flower stand once again. Detlev found the passageway. Detlev found the door frame of the dormitory door. Detlev heard Odel breathing, Xaver breathing, Alfred breathing. Detlev found his bed. The blanket was warmer than his skin.

— I don't want to go to pee alone at night.

Erwin jumped at him from behind the stair and shouted:
— Not on me. Not on me.
— How could the beam of light terrify King Herod so much?

The Christ Child grew a beard in four months. A few months after he had lain in the crib he was turning green and blue on the cross and frightening everyone who saw him, as Erwin again and again frightened Detlev.

There was the Christ Child. There was the angry Christ Child. The angry Christ Child was the cross-shaped beam of light from the young English women's projector. The angry Christ Child was the Easter Lamb with the ribbon.

— Why is the Christ Child so angry and why doesn't he catch the bombs in a big steel net over Munich?

Why does he allow people to become bad like Alfred and Joachim-Devil?

The beam of light over King Herod's bed was like the snow. One could sledge on the snow.

Detlev didn't dare think the rest. He sees himself going to the lavatory in the dark once more. Every second he expected that he would knock his toe against something, that he would cut his foot, that something would strike him down from behind.

He has already thought it, as he thinks:

— I mustn't think that.

If the orphanage children were to shape the Christ Child from snow, then it would melt away in the spring like all snowmen with a carrot for a nose, coals for buttons and eyes, with a crooked top hat on their heads.

— Detlev, open your eyes. Detlev, don't stand there like a wooden post. Your mother has crossed the church square below. Quickly wash your hands.

Quickly:

They were eating ice cream. Detlev was finished before his mother. She gave him the rest of hers.

— I want to leave.

— Now don't start that again.

— I want to leave.

— Don't go on.

— If we don't go away, I want to die.

— What kind of nonsense is that? We'll certainly die, if we go away from here.

— But perhaps no bomb will fall on our heads.

— Not just because of a bomb.

— The orphanage children asked me if I'm a Jew.

— When did they ask you that?

— What is a Jew?

— Don't say that word out loud. When did they ask you that? Who asked you that?

— I don't know any more. It was a long time ago.

— Why didn't you tell me?

— I don't know. They said, you'll be happy if I die.

— Perhaps mummy will start to cry now. Perhaps she'll say: No. Perhaps she'll hit me.

His mother looked at him. All that remained of her eyes was two black hoops with two round grey discs.

She got up. She crossed the street. She went as far as the edge of the town. She unlocked the front door. She unlocked the door to the room under the roof tiles of rabbit flesh. She reached out for Detlev, pulled him into her room. She locked the door.

— Detlev, don't interrupt me. I'm going to talk to you for a long time now – as if I'm reading you a fairy tale. But it isn't a fairy tale and if you love me you must tell no one else. – Your father is Jude – a Jew.

Detlev saw a great golden J. Birds sat on the cross-beam of the letter and sang. The apples ripened, the plums and the greengages. The U was the Elbe in the sunshine. The U was full of water. Golden steamers sailed across the U. Seagulls flew over it, and smoke rose from the locomotives on the Elbe Bridge. Uncle Bruno's car stopped in front of the Elbe tunnel.

The hydrangeas in the front garden at six in the morning, wet and golden, were the D and the E.

— Your father is a Jew. He lived nearby. He had to flee, before we got married.

Detlev didn't ask:

— Why did he have to flee? How did he flee? What does flee mean? Detlev saw Kriegel running down the crooked path. In the distance, fled a little man.

Detlev took Kriegel away again. Lots of dogs ran down the crooked path: Detlev took the dogs away again. Lots of people ran down the crooked path: Mrs Schwartz, Mrs Kwasniak, Mr Juskowiak, Mrs Selge, Mr Selge, Paul Selge, Mr and Mrs Wiesnagrotzki.

Detlev took the crooked path away again.

— I don't know if he got to Sweden safely. Thank God, I don't have his name and you don't have his name.

— What's he called?

— Something ending in Schritzki. Didn't I tell you that once before? You don't need to know it. It's lucky that no one knows it.

— What is a Jew?

Detlev saw large, broad, fat men with white baggy breeches and white fur-trimmed jackets drawing nearer. They swung long swords through the air. They had shining blue eyes long brown beards. They sang in deep voices.

— A Jew is someone who doesn't like to wash himself, who is untidy and shuffles along as he walks, who doesn't stand up straight, Detlev, and who turns his feet inwards when he sits down – they say. You're a half Jew.

— Yes.

— What does yes mean? Never say yes. No one knows. If someone asks you a question, to set a trap for you, never say yes. So you're a half Jew. Come closer. In Hamburg no one really knows, because they can't tell from our names. It can't be in any documents, I wasn't married to him. When we were evacuated, no inquiries had begun about us yet. They wouldn't have let us escape otherwise. Only, someone at the office made an insinuation. There was time enough to go to Bavaria. It takes a long time for an alteration to be entered in the documents and for the documents to be sent here from department to department.

— What will we do, when they arrive here?

— They're not here yet. At any rate no decision has been taken against us. Only Gemsheim dropped a remark once and Mrs Karl too. It also became more and more difficult to get a room.

— Then the documents are already here.

— No. Don't say that!

— Let's go to Hamburg. You said yourself it takes a long time for the documents to be sent on. In Hamburg we'll be safe for a long time. And when the documents come back to Hamburg, perhaps a bomb will fall on them and no one will be able to read them any more.

If there had been no doll's eye, there would be no orphanage, there would be no box of building bricks, which looks like the orphanage. There wouldn't be the other box full of cubes, with which one can put together landscapes.

Hamburg existed. How long would Hamburg exist?

Detlev would never have come to the orphanage. Erwin wouldn't exist, Erwin who on Easter Monday still shouted:

— Not on me.

Erwin, who imitated the wounded soldier, who wouldn't exist, who played Herod, who would never have existed, who feared the beam of light, which was nothing, which stood for the angry Christ Child, who could melt away like a snowman. Not even the tin Christ Child in the fish tank would exist, not a single pole for a scaffolding, no bell, no building block for a stairway. Siegfried wouldn't exist twice over. The red ribbon of the Easter Lamb in the churchyard wouldn't exist. Everything would be black. The snow would not look white. There would be nothing. There would be nothing at all.

Detlev looks down at himself. His feet disappear, his knees, his stomach, one button after another, his hands, the bird dropping on them, the nose in the middle in front of his eyes. Detlev lets his eyelids shut. Between closing and re-opening his head disintegrates; a last small chamber is all that is left of Detlev, smaller than his eye-sockets or than his auricles. The one sentence grows longer. Detlev slowly squeezes it through the last small chamber, which remains of himself, just as his grandmother squeezed raspberries through the linen cloth. He sees himself playing the recorder. He names the notes.

— C,C,A,C,C,A,B,G,B,A,C,C.

Very slowly, with swollen fingers, he takes one letter after another out of the letter case.

The words 'there' and 'would' and 'be' blur. He clearly hears the word 'nothing' and the word 'at' and the word 'all' in the last corner that is left of his body. He hears the lips of a gigantic mouth parting. He hears saliva splashing against the teeth, as the N, the O, the T, the H, the I, the N, the G, the A, the T, the A, the L, the L are pronounced.

The voices become confused:

— Nothing would exist.

— Hamburg exists.

— Scheyern wouldn't exist.

— Quickly.

Before his mother comes, before he has to go to the wash basin.

He hears himself saying:

— Look, your mother's coming.

He hears:

—. . .would exist.

— Sister Silissa will say:

Look your mother's coming.

— Detlev, there's your mother.

— They think mummy will give everyone sweets.

As Detlev sees the words 'nothing would' quite clearly in front of him made up of the letters from the school letter case, he sees above them, coloured red, a big H, a small B, a small G.

— That's how grandad writes Hamburg.

At the word 'nothing' he thinks:

— Not even the smallest lump of my head, over which my eyes at least could still close. In that tiny lump I can hear everything, and I can see myself running back and forward between Scheyern and Hamburg. I can see my father in it and the Jews.

Nothing would be left of my head. There would be nothing at all. I wouldn't exist.

Simultaneously:

— Mummy's coming, you're a dummy.

He sees once more a small E, and a small X, and a small I, and a small S, and a small T, as well as half a bicycle from the town moat, the toys, the instruments of martyrdom of the three hovering women.

When he hears 'Exist' and 'Your mother's coming' and 'Sister Silissa will say: Your mother's coming,' he sees Karl Street in Lokstedt, a Christmas tree like the ones the Anglo–Americans dropped and a fir tree of Meccano parts and the entrance to Hagenbeck's Zoo.

When the words 'would exist' appear and the red Hbg, hair falls down over a candle. He sees a second bicycle and two boxes of building bricks in the middle of Karl Street.

— There would be nothing at all.

Cellophane pictures with the Virgin Mary, cellophane pictures with the house and the Führer are blown away over the church tower by the sound of the siren. The backdrops for the Christmas play are reflected on a silver bauble and, on the side facing Detlev, the distorted rocks with the Risen Christ, cardboard rocks with penguins and a pink sugar lamb and seagulls and wounded soldiers.

— I wouldn't exist.

Detlev opens his eyes again.

The Christmas bauble shatters.

The group of orphanage children emerges behind the thin shards.

— Don't fall over, Detlev.

— Don't rub the bird shit on your suit.

— Detlev, your eyes are shining. Your cheeks are unnaturally red.

— Have you got a temperature, Detlev?

— Say something.

— Go and wash your hands, so that you don't have to greet your mother with dirty hands.

The singing dropped down from the very top, out of the stone rhubarb leaves. The singing was made up of several voices: one squeaking, one sour, one high, one red.

Below, the bearded Christ figure arose among the cardboard rocks. Above, the voices drew circles, lilies, chalices among the grey filaments.

Detlev grew cool from the singing. The singing turned deep red. It ran down Detlev. Detlev wished he had wings, to be able to fly up, towards the beginning of the singing.

His mother has stepped through the dining room door, has passed the soup pots, the tables covered with plates, forks, spoons.

She has put up her hair for the journey.

Detlev runs towards her. He touches his face. His face is smeared. He's frightened. He doesn't dare say what he's done. His mother doesn't notice it.

Sister Appia and Sister Silissa don't know what to do. Now that his mother has arrived, they don't want to intervene any more. They won't say anything more about washing. Detlev sees them deliberately press their lips together, as he turns towards them away from his mother.

His mother exists.

Sister Silissa and Sister Appia and Alfred and Frieda and Shaky exist.

They exist for the last time. Their eyes won't look at him for much longer. He won't see their eyes for much longer.

Only his mother and grandad and grandma and Hamburg will be left.

He hears his mother say:

— Shake everyone's hand before you leave.

He doesn't see the hands clearly. Higher. Lower. Alfred's hand, which only half takes his because of the bird dropping. Detlev doesn't want to lose any time. He's glad that no one reminds him of washing downstairs, where the cloths hang over the tub. He's glad that his mother hasn't noticed his dirty hands. He's pleased that the orphanage children only offer half a reluctant hand as he leaves. That makes it quicker. Erwin's hand. Odel's cold, damp, fat hand. Only the pinkie of Joachim-Devil's hand. Frieda's hand – without the little roll of paper from which he could have read the prayers of conversion. He's afraid that she might bend down to whisper the long difficult prayer to him, and then force him to repeat it once again, before he can go away. She would correct him, go back to the beginning again, until he had remembered it.

He doesn't look up at Frieda.

Little Xaver's hand jerks away.

Still more hands, that he no longer wants to distinguish. Hands that could be missing. Thirty-five or thirty-seven hands. Hands that quickly reach out to him and fall back again.

Sister Silissa's hand with the ring. Sister Silissa kisses him on the forehead. The little drop of spittle grows cold on the skin.

Detlev stands on the orphanage balcony. He looks over towards the church yard. The Easter Lamb's red ribbon still lies on the plot of grass beside the apse. It had been left lying there when the sacristan's son broke off the sugar lamb's head to eat it up. Detlev is waiting for his mother. Before she comes to fetch him, he is to eat supper with all the orphanage children for the last time. But his mother comes too early. She crosses the church square below as the nuns stir two eggs into the two big soup pots. Detlev discovers a doll's eye on a buttress. He wants to pinch it between his fingers and lift it up. It's not a doll's eye, but a bird dropping, which is smeared over Detlev's fingertips. The orphanage children notice the bird dropping on Detlev's hands. Sister Appia and Sister Silissa step out onto the balcony. They tell Detlev to wash his hands. Detlev is ashamed. He wishes the bird dropping away. He wishes everything away. He wishes himself away. He opens and shuts his eyes. Quickly. He blinks. He begins to sweat. The pictures blur into his surroundings on the balcony. He breathes more slowly and more quickly. He believes he's flying. He raises his hands. He begins to wipe them clean.

In his memory he muddles up the different parts of the year. He smells what has already passed. He stretches his thumb away from his hand. The threads of bird dropping between his fingers break.

Each twitch of his eyelashes lasts a whole day, a whole week, a whole month.

He thinks of his grandfather's garden.

He's afraid his mother has forgotten their departure.

Detlev's perceptions quicken. He remembers parts of movements, individual sounds. His lips twitch, as if he wanted once more to pronounce the words that have passed. Detlev looks down from the balcony again. But his mother has already passed through the main door below. Detlev's thoughts skip past more quickly. They jump back and forward between Scheyern, Aichach, Steingriff, Lokstedt. His mother stands in front of him. Before he has remembered everything, before he has wished away everything – all but the tiny brain chamber, out of which his thoughts come. It too disappears in the end.

His mother exists.

Hamburg exists.

Detlev wants to build a solid house for his mother in Lokstedt, which no one can knock down like a house of building blocks.

Frieda doesn't give him the prayer of conversion.

Sister Silissa kisses him on the forehead. The little drop of spittle grows cold on the skin.

— My father is as tall as the clouds, thinks Detlev as he goes out.

Detlev's mother takes his suitcase. They walk past Saint Joseph's Fountain in the direction of the station. Detlev draws away from the God in the orphanage.

GLOSSARY

Feldherrnhalle: A neo-classical building in Munich housing statues of famous Bavarian generals

Fieseler-Storch: A German reconnaissance plane

Gauleiter: In Nazi Germany, the Nazi Party official in charge of a province

Giant Mountains (Riesengebirge): Range between Bohemia and Silesia

Lenbach Museum: Lenbach Street etc: Places in Munich

Lokstedt and Eimsbüttel: Districts of Hamburg

Odel: Familiar form of Otto in Bavaria

Reich Field Marshal: i.e. Hermann Goering, commander of the German air force

Richtkranz: A garland placed to mark the erection of the roof timbers of a house

Sepp: Familiar form of Joseph

Stuka (Abbr. for Sturzkampfflugzeug): A German dive bomber

Winter Relief Fund (Winterhilfswerk): A Nazi welfare charity organization

Rübezahl: A sprite

The Piano Teacher
Elfriede Jelinek

'A bravura performance.'

SHENA MACKAY, *Sunday Times*

'Good books, like haircuts, should fill you with awe, change your life, or make you long for another. Elfriede Jelinek's *The Piano Teacher* manages to fulfil at least two of these demands in a reckless recital that is difficult to read and difficult to stop reading. The racy, relentless, consuming style is a metaphor for passion: impossible to ignore.'

CAROLE MORIN, *New Statesman & Society*

'Something of a land-mine . . . a brilliant, deadly book.' ELIZABETH J. YOUNG, *City Limits*

'Some may see, in the pain of this novel, its panic and its deep despair, a model of current writing. For others, *The Piano Teacher* will remain a perverse horror story of a mother's love taken to its logical, deadly extreme.'

ANGELA MCROBBIE, *The Independent*

288 pages £7.95 (paper)

The Passport
Herta Müller

'A haunting and original novel that's both satire and elegy.' MICHÈLE ROBERTS, *City Limits*

'Herta Müller's language is the purest poetry. Every sentence has the rhythm of poetry, indeed is a poem or a painting.' *Nürnberger Nachrichten*

'Each short chapter has a title like a poem, and that is precisely what they are, cantos, prose poems, rhythmic texts.' *Neue Zürcher Zeitung*

96 pages £4.95 (paper)

Also published by Serpent's Tail

Dreaming of Dead People
Rosalind Belben

'Rosalind Belben's eye for the movement and texture of the natural world is extraordinarily acute and she has a poet's ear for language. Her book, although apparently a cry of loneliness and deprivation, is also a confession of fulfilment, of endless curiosity for, and love of, life.' SELINA HASTINGS, *The Daily Telegraph*

'Her heroine is a solitary woman who is suffering as she reconciles herself to loneliness and sterility. She tells of her past and recalls, often, the countryside, where being alone is not painful and, if there is no meaning to life, the call to the senses is immediate. The book is beautifully written . . . it will not, repeat *not*, make an acceptable Christmas gift for a person living alone.' HILARY BAILEY, *The Guardian*

'So extraordinarily good that one wants more, recognizing a writer who can conjure an inner life spirit, can envisage, in unconnected episodes, a complete world: one unified not by external circumstances but by patterns of the writer's mind.'
ISABEL QUIGLY, *The Financial Times*

'Some of the most memorable prose in contemporary fiction.' LINDA BRANDON, *The Independent*

'Rosalind Belben's gift or burden is to press on to the painful edge of what is possible. It is an achievement to celebrate.' MAGGIE GEE, *The Observer*

176 pages £6.95 (paper)

Is Beauty Good
Rosalind Belben

'A startling record of life preserved in the face of increasing desolation . . . Rosalind Belben's gift or burden is to press on to the painful edge of what is possible. It is an achievement to celebrate.'

MAGGIE GEE, *The Observer*

'In her work Belben gives us glimpses of such beauty that one can only choose, like her, to celebrate life.'

LINDA BRANDON, *The Independent*

'Spare, lucid prose, reminiscent of Woolf's *The Waves.*'   *The Guardian*

'Belben has an ability to tap deeply into the process of thought itself with all its fragmentation, puns, jokes, obscenities and moments of transfiguration . . . In this case beauty is certainly good.'

ELIZABETH J. YOUNG, *City Limits*

128 pages £6.95 (paper)

Marks of Identity
Juan Goytisolo

'For me *Marks of Identity* was my first novel. It was forbidden publication in Spain. For twelve years after that everything I wrote was forbidden in Spain. So I realized that my decision to attack the Spanish language through its culture was correct. But what was most important for me was that I no longer exercised censorship on myself, I was a free writer. This search for and conquest of freedom was the most important thing to me.'

Juan Goytisolo, in an interview with *City Limits*

'Juan Goytisolo is by some distance the most important living novelist from Spain ... and *Marks of Identity* is undoubtedly his most important novel, some would say the most significant work by a Spanish writer since 1939, a truly historic milestone.'

The Guardian

'A masterpiece which should whet the appetites of British readers for the rest of the trilogy.'

Times Literary Supplement

352 pages £8.95 (paper)

Also published by Serpent's Tail

Landscapes After the Battle
Juan Goytisolo

'Juan Goytisolo is one of the most rigorous and original contemporary writers. His books are a strange mixture of pitiless autobiography, the debunking of mythologies and conformist fetishes, passionate exploration of the periphery of the West – in particular of the Arab world which he knows intimately – and audacious linguistic experiment. All these qualities feature in *Landscapes After the Battle*, an unsettling, apocalyptic work, splendidly translated by Helen Lane.'   MARIO VARGAS LLOSA

'*Landscapes After the Battle* . . . a cratered terrain littered with obscenities and linguistic violence, an assault on "good taste" and the reader's notions of what a novel should be.'   *The Observer*

'Fierce, highly unpleasant and very funny.'
The Guardian

'A short, exhilarating tour of the emergence of pop culture, sexual liberation and ethnic militancy.'
New Statesman

'Helen Lane's rendering reads beautifully, capturing the whimsicality and rhythms of the Spanish without sacrificing accuracy, but rightly branching out where literal translation simply does not work.'
Times Literary Supplement

176 pages £7.95 (paper)

Forties' Child
Tom Wakefield

'Through his detailed, accurate and incisive obser-
vances and remembrances there exudes a natural
unforced sentiment which proves both genuinely
heartwarming and eminently readable ... It's one of
those books that cannot be put down, and once
finished demands to be read again.'   *Time Out*

'Beautifully evoked, touching and immensely readable.'   *Gay Times*

'He is able to touch base with the reader somewhere
at some time and you know exactly what he means
and why it is so important.'   *City Limits*

'A tender and original recollection of the way a child
puts the amazing world together.'
                     EDMUND BLISHEN, *The Guardian*

'I greatly enjoyed Tom Wakefield's classic autobio-
graphical account of a wartime Midlands boyhood.'
                        BEL MOONEY, *The Times*

'What disarmingly polished scenes they are. Tom
Wakefield is one of our most engaging of novelists.'
                  VALENTINE CUNNINGHAM, *TLS*

176 pages £5.95 (paper)

The Variety Artistes
Tom Wakefield

'Wakefield possesses a keen sense of drama and draws some wonderful, almost theatrical "scenes" which can be re-read, enjoyed and savoured, and his characters are full-bodied, living creations who quickly become familiar and memorable. Warm, sensitive and witty.' *Time Out*

'A lovely story . . . a gentle, humorous parable that says: Watch out — given the chance, there could be a lot more to that compliant old woman than meets the eye.' *New Society*

'Full of humour, tenderness, humanity and confidence in life.' *Gay Scotland*

'Somewhat picaresque, intensely human, richly comic, *The Variety Artistes* is an absorbing and ultimately deeply moving novel.' *Gay Times*

192 pages £6.95 (paper)

Who Was That Man?
A Present for Mr Oscar Wilde
Neil Bartlett

'. . . touching and exasperating, it makes an elegant and intelligent shelfmate to Richard Ellmann's biography. Whether or not you appreciate it may give a good indication of how you would really have felt about Wilde himself.' *TLS*

'Always intelligent, often moving but never sentimental, this is a book which is at once critical of, and beautifully sensitive to, gay culture.' *Gay Times*

'This is an extraordinary book. Part detective story, part literary criticism, part social history and part confessional, this "present for Mr Oscar Wilde" reveals what it is like to be gay in a city that, for the most part, pretends you don't exist.' *i-D*

'A reflection on the links between gay lives today and those of Oscar Wilde, his friends, lovers and acquaintances.' *Capital Gay Book of the Year*

256 pages £9.95 (paper) illustrated

The Life of the Automobile
Ilya Ehrenburg

'A Futurist-Expressionist masterpiece, superbly translated.' *Sunday Times*

'A revelation.' ALAN BRIEN, *New Statesman*

'A valuable historical document and an interesting exploration of the ground between analysis and the "fictional" narrative . . . readable and gripping.'
HUW BEYNON, *New Society*

176 pages £5.95 (paper)